DATE DUE	
MAY 1 2 1994		
JAN 05 1995		
Invermere Publ.b		
due: 14Sep09		

TAXI!

TAXI!

HELEN POTREBENKO

NEW STAR BOOKS
VANCOUVER
1989

Canadian Cataloguing in Publication Data

Potrebenko, Helen, 1940–
    Taxi!

First ed. published 1975.
ISBN 0-919573-89-4

    I. Title.
PS8581.076T3 1989   C813'.54   C89-091123-1
PR9199.3.P67T3 1989

The publisher is grateful for assistance provided by
the Canada Council, and by the Cultural Services Branch,
Province of British Columbia.

First published 1975.
Reprinted 1975, 1977.
Second, revised edition published June 1989.

Printed and bound in Canada.
1 2 3 4 5   93 92 91 90 89

New Star Books Ltd.
2504 York Avenue
Vancouver, B.C.
Canada V6K 1E3

TAXI!

One Sunday morning in December, Shannon sat on the Carrall stand for half an hour before she decided that the Columbia stand would be busier. The despatcher called the Carrall as she drove away and Shannon saw 91 pull onto the stand just in time to take the call. She clicked her microphone in frustration and drove down Hastings towards the Columbia.

When she stopped at the red light, signalling to turn left, she saw that there was a woman lying on the Columbia stand. Along the edge of the sidewalk, a muddy rivulet of water ran down to Hastings. The woman was lying on the sidewalk with her face hanging in the spit and vomit-soaked water. About the time the light turned green, two men picked up the woman and seated her on the sidewalk. One of them wiped her face with his handkerchief and then they both went away.

Shannon pulled onto the stand and stopped beside the woman, being careful not to drive over her feet. The woman stared straight ahead at Shannon because Shannon was directly in her line of vision.

Are you all right? Shannon asked.

I'm okay.

Are you sure?

I'm okay.

Did you fall?

Yes.

Are you drunk?

Yes.

Where were you going?

I'm looking for my purse. I lost my purse.

Where?

I don't know.

She was an Indian woman of an age somewhere between 15 and 50. Her face was puffy and appeared flattened out. One eye was swollen and blue and there was a partially healed cut across one side of her forehead. She sat quietly on the spit-dirtied sidewalk of Columbia Street, not seeing any of it.

Do you live around here? Shannon asked.

Yes.

Why don't you go home and sleep for a few hours and then look for your purse?

(At this time in her history as a cab-driver, Shannon still thought drunk people who fell down could be fixed up by a few hours sleep.)

Maybe I should, the woman said.

Can I drive you somewhere?

I've got no money. It was in my purse.

That's okay. I'll drive you anyway.

No. I'm okay.

Did you hurt your head just now?

What?

You have a cut across your head and a black eye.

Somebody beat me up.

Is your head hurt?

No. I'm okay.

You haven't been drinking, Shannon said accusingly.

No. Not today.

It's your head that's hurt and that's why you fell.

Somebody beat me up.

I'll take you to a hospital.

No.

No, better not. Better that she go and find another drink since what was wrong with her was not so much connected with drunkenness as with sobriety. But Shannon only learned this later. That day, with the woman staring at her, she insisted without success that a hospital would be a good place to go.

I'm okay, the woman kept saying.

Look, Shannon said angrily, if you don't look after yourself you're going to die.

That's good, the woman said in the same flat voice, staring unwaveringly straight ahead.

The first time Shannon drove cab drunk out of her mind was the Christmas after the War Measures Act. The passengers were also mostly pissed out of their minds and vacillated between desperate gaiety and irrational rage. A driver called for the cops in front of the Peter Pan and in the background was the sound of a woman sobbing.

At the B and G stand, Shannon got into Frank Anchuk's car and asked him if it would be busy. Naw, he said, just some hypocrites going to church and drunks going somewhere to get drunker.

Shannon was sober on Boxing Day at 5 a.m. when a man flagged her on Smithe Street. Where can I buy a girl? he asked. Shannon gassed the car at him but he was on the sidewalk and she didn't drive up on the sidewalk. Girls can't be bought like cattle, she screamed.

She drove to the Davie stand and found Buzz Ahonen already sitting there so she got in the back seat of his car. Do you want any coffee? Buzz didn't. A man came walking along, peered into the back seat, and started opening the door. You got a fare, Shannon told Buzz, getting out the other side. But then the man followed her to her car. You looking for a cab? Shannon asked. No, for a girl. Go fuck yourself, you pig, girls can't be bought like cattle. Buzz didn't have anything to drink so after the next fare, Shannon went home and drank to the silent morning. By the time she was on the street again, the sun was coming up and the morning dissolved into a red mist.

New Year's was about like that too. There were drunks crawling all over the streets at 5 a.m., assaulting her with their feverish gaiety. Several people passed out in the car, causing no end of trouble. There was a no-pick-up order because they were so busy, but a strong young man got in the car at a light. Shannon explained he had to get out because of the no-pick-up order.

Tell the despatcher it's Zaza, the young man said. Shannon told the despatcher it was Zaza and the despatcher said okay.

We're all god's children, a guy in a stupid hat told her over and over again. He looked like if he stopped saying it, the desperate gaiety would crack and he would disappear into a void, leaving only the hat behind. We're all god's children.

We're all god's children, Shannon told Gerald when she found him in the bus depot cafe. He shouldn't screw around so much. Overpopulation. And a Happy New Year to you.

It is New Year's?

Didn't you know?

I did, actually. I was walking down Granville and all the stores were closed so I thought it must be New Year's. Or Christmas.

Christmas was a week ago. Do you want a drink?

No.

Good thing, too. It sure causes problems. After the revolution, we'll have public washrooms. The worst problem about being a cabbie is not having anywhere to pee. How do you manage, you people walking around the streets?

It's easier for men.

Oh yeah, the men cabbies stop in a lane. The other worst problem is . . .

But she didn't tell him the other problem, only asked him if he wanted a drink, which he again refused. The problem was the bellyache and you couldn't talk to men about that, because it was due to chronic sexual frustration. Those were the bad years, and about the only time Shannon wasn't horny was when there were men around. Men are trained all their lives to hate sex, and they learn to confuse sex with violence and most often use it as a form of power with which to insult women. Since it is only a power trip, men are interested in the prelude to sex and very often are incapable of fucking at all, or of enjoying it when they do. It's enough to turn off even the most frustrated of females. Thus Shannon tried unsuccessfully to persuade herself that women didn't have any sex drive, and took 222s for the pain in her belly.

Gerald explained that serious dope smokers didn't drink, so

she gave him $5 to buy dope with and he was too polite to tell
her it wasn't enough. She had a few more drinks and went home.
Feeling benevolent, she staggered up the stairs to see Bradley
and Evelyn. They didn't seem too pleased to see her, but the baby did. After the baby's effusive greeting, the three adults chat-
ted amicably and even drank a toast of friendship in the New
Year. But then she told them about Gerald and they had a stupid
argument about whether or not middle-class kids had the right
to drop out, with Shannon arguing it wasn't really a choice. The
whole time they were arguing, Gerald was walking and it was the
middle of winter and raining. He walked and walked, huddled
inside the faded and dirty jacket which had once cost $89. Or sat
for hours nodding over a single cup of coffee in some all-night
joint. It was such a long night and there were so many nights and
he would have thought about poetry if his feet didn't hurt.

When Bradley and Evelyn discovered that Shannon had
loaned him money they were really furious and told her she was
beyond help, even though she assured them Gerald would pay it
back. Then she got into a drunken rage and thought how much
she sounded like all her passengers, and didn't speak to Bradley
or Evelyn again until after the baby was talking.

She told Gerald she hated them and would move out if she
could afford to. The truth was she didn't want to move. In the
night she could listen to Bradley singing, or hear the intense
love in Evelyn's voice when she talked to the baby, and the baby
laughing.

Shannon always thought times were bad, but it was about 1968
when the bad times really started.

The war in Vietnam had been going on for many years by
then, and the protests all over the world had no visible effect so
that they diminished and all but disappeared in the next few
years. In 1968 the Russian army marched into Czechoslovakia,

destroying finally whatever illusions people still had about the other empire being better.

Shannon and Bradley lost their jobs about the same time the following year. Shannon's was the usual personality conflict and it hadn't been much of a job to lose, so she didn't worry about it. For Bradley, who had been replaced by a machine in the bottling factory, the situation was much more difficult. He had just had a baby and Evelyn refused to look for a job, proclaiming that Bradley wasn't capable of looking after a tiny baby. Evelyn didn't know how to look after a tiny baby either, but armed with Dr. Spock and complete faith in motherhood, she felt vastly superior to Bradley in the matter. Her faith in motherhood gradually diminished as the baby cried from colic for hours and didn't gain weight properly. Nevertheless, she remained convinced that the baby would have done worse under Bradley's care.

Bradley finally got a job doing something in the power plant at SFU. Shannon didn't think it sounded like any hell, but he liked it and didn't have to work very hard and came home happy enough to sing songs to the baby when she cried from colic for three months.

It didn't last long. B.C. Tel employees were on strike, and one morning they set up a picket at the bottom of the SFU hill. Bradley didn't cross it and was fired for not coming to work. He didn't worry, thinking that the union would see he was re-hired, but they only laughed and said they hadn't expected anyone to honour that picket line. So then Bradley went to talk to the students, but they were too busy talking about workers to cater to the problems of a mere worker. After several weeks of talking, Bradley realized he wasn't going to get his job back. He drank more after that, but he still sang songs to the baby.

Now that the baby was bigger and had begun to laugh, Evelyn got a job as a medical receptionist, which paid almost enough to live on, and Bradley stayed home with the baby. He sang songs and fed her, which he liked doing, and he also changed her diapers, which he didn't like doing.

Shannon bought a new dress and stockings and went job-hunting. She filled out 19 applications and had five interviews and came home crying after each one. After the fifth one, she threw the stockings in the garbage and sobbed to Evelyn that she would starve to death sooner than face another interview. None of the five interviews turned into a job.

Why didn't you ever learn to type? Evelyn asked. I can type. I've got stiff fingers, Shannon sobbed. Everyone acts as if typing is easy, but it isn't.

Evelyn sat around waiting patiently until she quit crying, then told her to go back to university, whereupon Shannon burst into tears again. They were all planning to go to university when Bradley's aunt left him the house. All three of them. Going to university was how you made it. University is the $10,000 difference in your life. Or is it $50,000? The house was really old and the basement leaked and they had to pay exorbitant lawyer's fees for the transfer. They pooled all their money, thinking they had it made anyhow since they'd never have to pay rent. But things were always going wrong and the taxes went up and Bradley and Evelyn had a baby. Shannon was the only one to get to university and she didn't last long.

Evelyn, when we were young, it was going to be so easy, Shannon sobbed. Are we getting old that it gets more difficult each day?

I don't know. You're the one who always knew things.

Things have changed.

Shannon had driven cab part-time before; now she went back to driving full-time. She still owed $1,867.43 plus $250.56 interest from the student loans, and the collectors were a bit upset about it. The cab company assured her the wages of a spare driver couldn't be garnisheed and that they never revealed drivers' names or addresses to anyone. About then the old furnace broke down and neither Bradley nor Evelyn could do anything about it, so Bradley borrowed the money, and Shannon undertook the payments. It was still cheaper than paying rent.

Remember when I had that good job? she asked Evelyn. I quit. You should never quit a job. But I guess we were victimized by the rising expectations of the 50s. We were kind of naive, eh? We were going to be somebody. Well, now I'm somebody all right.

She got blind drunk a number of times all by herself in the basement, and then had an awful fight with Bradley followed by an awful fight with Evelyn. Even though they weren't speaking to each other, she felt she could continue living in the same house because she had put so much money into it. In the evening, lying on her bed, she could hear Bradley singing and the baby laughing.

She drank, but not as much as she feared she would. She lost track of all her old friends and didn't make any new ones except for Gerald. She didn't mind losing friends, was the truth of the matter, and she didn't mind not speaking to Evelyn and Bradley. You never know who your friends will turn out to be. She thought it was better to be alienated and arrogant, and it's easier to play at arrogance with people you don't like. Still, even the most alienated and arrogant need one friend.

She would have preferred a woman friend but she hardly ever met any women. Few cab-drivers are women and few women earn enough money to ride in cabs much. She met Gerald on the Davie stand. She was sitting there on a rainy Sunday morning at 4 o'clock. (Women weren't allowed to drive nights so the company decreed 3:30 a.m. to be morning.) A young man stopped by the window. She opened the door for him, thinking he was a fare, but he explained apologetically he only wanted directions to the youth hostel. She told him the youth hostel wasn't open until later in the day. He said he wasn't going there, only asking directions. He was shivering from the cold so she asked him to sit in the car for a while. He was terribly grateful and asked what he could do in return, so she gave him 30 cents and sent him back out in the rain to buy some coffee. (You could buy coffee for 15 cents in the old days.) He went to the Chick and Bull and then came back to sit in the cab and drink coffee.

Gerald was a petit bourgeois dispossessed son. He said he was learning to live on the streets. It was the wrong time of year to do that, as most street people go home in winter and only live on the street in the summer, but Gerald did most things backwards. Shannon told him it was a stupid thing to do, winter or summer, and that he ought to get a job, so he asked her how to become a cab-driver and she got surly and said maybe he should live on the street after all. He was looking for reality and truth and poetry, which the propaganda of the day said could be found in dope and on the streets.

Taxi drivers have a lot of time to think on the job. Sexual fantasies occupy a lot of time. Then there's the dream of the Big Trip – the one that will pay them a whole lot of money all at once in some unexplained fashion. Some count their money endlessly or daydream about making it big in gambling or in business. They think about almost everything but pushing hack. Although Shannon, too, did her share of escape and sex fantasies, she found philosophising and politics more satisfying. Thus she could tell Gerald with the superiority and certainty of the armchair philosopher that the purpose of the hippie propaganda was to keep young people off the labour market.

Until the 1960s there had been growth in the manufacturing industries in Canada. This growth ceased, and in both primary and secondary industries, technology increased productivity. Thus a large proportion of young men were no longer required as workers. There was no war to send them to and historical developments precluded the bourgeois from gassing them, so any number of other strategies were devised. One was to increase the age of youth. Instead of being adults at 16, men were still considered children at 30. Universities increased and expanded to accommodate more students, and trades which had been learned by apprenticeship were now taught in technical schools. All this meant that men were kept off the labour market longer. The service industries continued to expand so that most women did not suffer, or benefit, from an equal extended training period.

Since young people with degrees soon discovered that they couldn't get jobs after waiting all those years either, there had to be further means devised to keep youth off the labour market. The most successful of these was the hippie philosophy.

Hippies benefited the bourgeoisie by staying off the labour market without complaining about it or causing trouble; they did this by believing they had thought it all up themselves. Further, by devising a distinctive style of dress, they isolated themselves from the regular workers and didn't muck up the work ethic. They could be pointed at and called different, and ordinary workers didn't think they also should stop working. Rather incidentally, hippies also started a whole new consumer market for rotting capitalism to benefit from. Ragged jeans, groovy shirts, and the like, as well as music, commercial revolution, and popularization of detachment. "Cool" was required to make sure they didn't cause trouble, and if they were required to join the work force after all, they should do so without any more indignation than accompanied being forced to stay away.

It all worked out beautifully and for those who like happy endings, it should be noted that recession and unemployment and inflation and war and devaluation bothered the ruling class not a bit and they remained rich.

For everybody else, it wasn't so great, but they didn't have the power to change anything. The streets acquired more people having nowhere to sleep. Despair and demoralization increased the crime rate and this was blamed on police laxness. Drunkenness and dope addiction increased by phenomenal numbers and more and more people took their own lives.

Capitalism had begun its cataclysmic degeneration. The U.S., defeated in Vietnam, continued bombing people in a manner indicating racism and fascism were gaining control and rational behaviour could no longer be expected.

In Canada there was the War Measures Act. Canadians woke up one morning to find all their civil rights had been taken away from them. English Canadians were soothed back to sleep again with the assurance that it wasn't meant for them, and that these laws would be used only on French Canadians. Ironically, it was the non-French who were terrified and became more compliant; some French-speaking people continued on their paths of defiance.

I used to think, Shannon told Gerald, that being a Canadian meant something.

But Gerald had been raised without dreams and had no illusions to shatter and didn't know what she was talking about. He sought meaning in dope and mysticism and thought himself an individual.

Fortunately, Shannon couldn't keep up the drinking for any length of time. For a while she hung around with Gracie who drove 35, but Gracie drank such enormous amounts that Shannon gave it all up, particularly after she lost $50 at the horse races. Gracie was fired for drinking and went to work for Chartreuse Taxi. Shannon met her for breakfast one morning and Gracie was enthusiastic about how much better Chartreuse was to work for, but then she didn't show up for any more breakfasts and Shannon never did find out what happened. Without women friends again, and sober, she continued driving.

On no, the large woman from the St. Helen's said. A woman! Do you want another cab?

No.

Where to?

Lake City.

Lake City?

Lake City.

Where is it?

Where is it???!!! The woman grasped the door handle as if to get out, but didn't get out.

Is it a hotel? Shannon asked.

Is it a hotel???!!!!

Look, if you want another cab, say so. If not, tell me where Lake City is.

Channel 8.

Channel 8?

Channel 8.

TV?

TV. Channel 8. Lake City.

Well, where is it?

You just go and I'll tell you.

Go where?

Lake City.

What street is it on?

You go down and turn at the Nabob sign.

Nabob sign where?

Lake City.

What street?

You a cab-driver and you don't know where Lake City is?

Look, lady, I already told you I didn't know where it was. People aren't born cab-drivers, you know. I do not know where every street and every building in Vancouver is.

It's not in Vancouver.

Ah! A clue! Where is it then?

Burnaby.

Burnaby. North or south?

You just go and I'll tell you.

Okay, now, slowly. Where do I start?

What?

Where do I begin to go so you can tell me where to go?

It's on the Lougheed Highway.

Why didn't you say so in the first place? Shannon said and started driving.

Where ya going! the woman yelped.

Cambie Bridge, Seventh Avenue, to Broadway.

Cambie?

Yes.

That isn't the way to Lake City.

It's the way to the Lougheed Highway. You said Lake City was on the Lougheed Highway.

You know the Lougheed Highway?

Like a brother.

Why are you going this way then?

Because it's the way to Lake City.

It isn't the way to Lake City.

Isn't Lake City on the Lougheed Highway?

Yes, but this isn't the way.

Lake City turned out to be almost in Coquitlam on the Lougheed Highway. Shannon was getting used to the fact that the people who got most indignant about cab-drivers getting lost were the ones who didn't know their way out of a wet paper bag. Once she had driven a young woman to a bank at which the woman had worked for two years without discovering what street it was on. She knew where to get off the bus but was unable to describe it to Shannon.

After successfully delivering the woman to her job at Lake City, Shannon drove all the way back through Burnaby and to zone 5 before she got another trip. It was a young man whose motorcycle wouldn't start due to the cold. When they got to where he worked, he discovered he had left his wallet at home and didn't have any money. Shannon gave him her car number and a card and he promised to drop the money off within a week. Shannon had been driving cab for some time already, but she was still a green driver and actually thought he would drop the money off.

She was really a stupid driver, as you will have noticed. The main indicator of her stupidity was the fact that she couldn't drink properly. A cabbie who stays sober is obviously stupid. At times of really gross stupidity, like when she thought a passenger would actually pay the fare, Shannon wondered how she had got where she was. She sometimes told fares they were riding with the stupidest driver in the entire city. How had she ended up as a driver?

Whenever Shannon told people about her early life, they told her she was laying trips on them and she didn't like laying trips on people.

Assume, then, that she was given birth to by a taxi. Fully-grown, sitting behind the wheel. They cut the cord and stuck a microphone at the nether end and that's how she came to be. The car was safe on cold winter mornings. She hated to leave the car even to get a coffee because a woman walking was subject to danger and ridicule whereas in the car she was safe. She was one of your sullen, garrulous, too expensive cab-drivers. They're all the same.

The older women got left over from the war when all drivers were women. The younger women got stuck there while on their way elsewhere. The two kinds have nothing in common except that they're tough.

The men have more in common with each other. That's because there are better jobs around for men and to some degree, they have a choice. All women's jobs are bad, so for a woman, it's a job like any other job.

Some of the men are recent immigrants and it's not true to say these men had a choice. They get into driving because it's hard for foreigners to get a job, and because it seems to them to be a good job at first. They get treated like dirt and at first this makes them overanxious and pathetically eager. But they soon discover that whatever they do, good or bad, they'll still be treated like dirt, so they become sullen and mean. They come from a lot of places: Italy, Hong Kong, the West Indies, India, Greece, Hungary, Czechoslovakia. You don't see any Americans driving cab. These men are all different from each other. It's the Canadian men who are stereotypes.

The young men are on their way up. Anybody can make it in this free, democratic, free enterprise, land of opportunity. For a

short time they'll be cabbies and then they'll have either com-
pleted their education or will have made the right contacts, and
then being a cabbie will be just a fun thing to look back on. A
few of them actually make it to bigger and better things, but they
look back only with bitterness.

Young men lie about the amount of money they make, and
think it is a romantic job. Strong as bulls, they do not yet suffer
the appalling fatigue, nor have their stomachs started rotting
from coffee and tension. It's all a party. Screaming around in a
high-powered car, ripping off drunks, screwing women, gathering in unruly gangs in fancy restaurants. It's all a party.

But the years go by and the party begins to get dull. They've
had a few accidents. They have discovered they get ripped off
much more often than they rip off. Their bodies break down fast
in the inhuman conditions under which they work. The traffic
gets worse every year. Fewer women are available for screwing
and none for loving. Now they drink less often, but more purposefully. Some must carry it around in a brown paper bag under
the seat, otherwise they can't make it through the day. They still
think pushing hack is a party and they think it's somehow their
own fault that they're not enjoying themselves any longer. They
don't think about it very much, and only occasionally take a
sober look at the diminishing sky and wonder how the hell it all
happened.

The old men know how it happened but they are too old to do
anything about it. Those who didn't learn to control their
drinking have now long disappeared into the crowd at Columbia
and Hastings.

Some of the ones who are still drivers are teetotalers. Others
have learned to control their drinking and stay carefully sober all
day, only at night sinking gratefully into drunken oblivion.
Sometimes they take days off because they have to cater to their
diminishing strength, and their needs have shrunk along with
the shrinking horizons. No more dreams. No more party. Only
the careful monotony occasionally breaking out into maniacal
bitterness. Now, finally, with the pride of manhood long broken, they will talk about how they got screwed.

Some of them got broken in other places – fishermen who went broke, loggers who had accidents, other men who couldn't stand the loneliness of many male occupations. Wherever they came from, they all suspect they might end up in the slums begging for a quarter. It has a terrible kind of attraction. Cabbies are the only people that Columbia and Hastings types can boss around, providing they have the price of a fare, so they ride in cabs quite often and are demanding and officious and thus survive a bit longer.

Owners are a whole different bunch. In the old days, drivers could eventually become owners, but by 1970 the price of a cab in Vancouver had risen to $30,000, and there is no way a driver will ever earn that kind of money.

Some of the owners are left over from the old days when drivers could still buy a cab and they aren't bad guys – slow, maybe, but considerate in a negative sort of way. A good owner is one who drives part of the week himself and therefore keeps the car in good working condition. He also never bothers the driver about anything and, preferably, has no communication with the driver at all.

Another kind of owner is the brand new one. He has borrowed money from his family to buy the cab and must now work 70 to 100 hours a week to pay it back. He hasn't got the money to fix or replace cars, and hates paying drivers at all, let alone deducting income tax or paying holiday pay as required by law.

About the same, or only slightly better, is the new owner coming from elsewhere. He has his own money, which he earned from some other job or business, but he doesn't have much and doesn't know much about the cab business and is niggardly and petty.

Absentee owners are retired or have inherited the cab from somewhere, and aren't very interested in it except for pocket money. They usually get a steady driver to look after the car but do not pay him extra for doing this.

The very worst kind of owner is the multiple car owner. He has anywhere from four to thirty cabs and these bring in a considerable amount of money without the owner doing anything at all. This money is most often invested in some other business, and the owner is not interested in his cabs except for the money they bring in. Curiously enough, these owners are even more niggardly than the poor owners and tend to terrorize drivers.

Labour laws are never enforced except against workers, so there is no protection for cab-drivers. This leads owners into excesses of abuse, and all the working conditions taken for granted by all other workers (except for farm workers and domestic labourers) are not available to cab-drivers. These are: the forty-hour week, eight-hour day, holidays, lunch breaks, income tax deductions, unemployment insurance, vacation pay, severance pay, minimum wage laws, safety regulations. About every four years, drivers attempt to form a union, at which time the aforementioned labour laws, which are never used on behalf of drivers, are used to prevent them from organizing.

Yet the problems of drivers are not caused by owners but by the nature of the society. With only a few exceptions, owners are just little guys trying to make a living. Most owners are themselves working under the same conditions as the drivers, though with a larger income. They are niggardly because they can't afford not to be, and it is difficult for drivers to hate them properly. If this was a decent society, all drivers would own the portion of the shift they drive.

None of which explains how Shannon got there. Not that an explanation is really necessary, as by now it must be obvious that hardly anyone would drive cab if she had another choice.

One day Shannon picked up two people at the MidCity Motel. One was an Indian man drinking from a bottle of beer; the other was his daughter, going to the hospital to get her cast changed. The man asked Shannon what kind of a job driving cab was and she told him it was shitty. He was a longshoreman but there weren't any jobs right then and it would be years before he got into the union. He talked about all the other jobs he hadn't been able to get.

Sure is hard to make a living when you're not a white man, he said, sipping on his beer.

Yep, Shannon agreed. Sure is hard to make a living when you're not a white man.

Every morning in the cab was pretty much like every other day. People climbed in and out. Mostly they said it was a nice day, then they commented on the fact that Shannon shouldn't be a woman, they wanted to know if she was married and they asked how the cab business was. Shannon answered few of these comments, as there really wasn't anything to say. Sometimes the drunks were a break in the monotony, but then they became a monotony themselves. They were all so alike.

Main Street, the drunk woman said.

Whereabouts on Main Street?

Just go to Main Street and I'll tell you where to stop.

Main is a long street, which end of it should I go to? Shannon smiled and was patient, the way one must be with mean drunks.

Huh?

Where on Main Street?

Finally the woman gave her a number. Shannon drove over the Georgia Viaduct and up Main.

Whyncha talkin? the drunk demanded.

Shannon shrugged. Nice day, eh?

I don't give a shit, the woman replied. After that she crouched silently in her corner. At the house, she turned to Shannon, smiling ingratiatingly. Ya mad at me?

Naw, why should I be mad? I ain't mad at anyone.

The woman got out and walked hurriedly into the house.

Shannon sighed. Christ, another one of those. She followed the woman into the house.

In one very crowded room there was a man and a woman and three children. The drunk had disappeared. The woman was lying in the bed, the man sat beside her, and the three little girls sat on the floor, all of them watching TV. When Shannon came in, the girls smiled at her. The man got to his feet.

Somebody owes me $1.85, Shannon said.

The children's smiles changed to expressions of fear. My mom? the biggest one asked.

Dunno. Was that your mom I brought?

Yeah.

Then your mom owes me $1.85.

The man had been digging in his pants pockets. He found there a ballpoint pen, a nickel, and two pennies, and offered it all to Shannon.

C'mon, she said irritably. You gotta do better'n that. I ain't working for nuthin.

The little girls ran into another room and Shannon could hear the littlest one crying. The man stood before her, hanging his head.

See, we're on welfare . . . he muttered, and waited limply for the verdict.

Shannon ran out of the house, slamming the door behind her.

We act like rats in a cage, snarling at each other over scraps, Shannon said to Gerald. The poor are supposed to be kind to the poor, but they don't seem to be. Behaviour is prescribed by economics, you know.

Yeah?

Yeah. Victims are horrible people. Suffering doesn't ennoble.

Why aren't my parents nice people then?

Oh, that's another problem. People who live off the backs of other people have to wear blinkers, otherwise they would see the nature of their lives and could no longer think of themselves as decent citizens. So they hide behind conventions and formality. That's what I like about owners. They're directly horrible because they have to be. After the revolution only the multiple owners will be shot, the rest won't even need rehabilitation.

So everybody lives the way they're told to.

The way they have to. Everybody most of the time. Not ever all the time. Hair style, clothing, manner of speech, ideas, cars, houses, and everything. Just like they have to. Even the way we walk. But not all the time. Comes a time when everybody breaks out. And that's the only characteristic of human nature I know of. Not greed, not obedience, not violence, nor any of those things the capitalists would have us believe are intrinsic. Only rebellion.

Nobody ever talked in the Drivers' Room. At first this irritated Shannon and she would make people talk. (Later, she too was silent and irritated by people who talked in the Drivers' Room.)

There I was, she said in the Drivers' Room to the backs of three drivers adding up their sheets, standing at the bottom of some very steep steps when this guy comes falling down them into my arms.

How romantic.

Yeah, so I led him down to the sidewalk, draped him over the car and asked where he wanted to go, and he didn't know.

Yeah? I lost $7.15 today . . .

So then he says if I'm worried about the money, he'll pay me right now, pulls out his wallet and it's empty. Then he tried to get into the cab and fell down. I draped him across the hood and called to see if anyone else wanted him. Twelve took him to Main and Broadway and took his watch, and left him a note in his pocket so that when he sobered up he could come and pay the $1.75 and get his watch back. Not that he'll ever see that fare. If you turn in securities and the fare redeems them, the manager, or the office staff, or the owner steals the money. Anyway, the driver never sees the money.

Hey, how come you got one at the airport? You're going to go to court for hustling fares out there.

I didn't. He hustled me. I went in to get coffee and when I came out, there's this guy waiting and I say, real virtuous, that I can't take him unless he phoned for a Purple Door. He says he phoned and climbs in and then starts telling me how much he hates them Blue bastards and they're all crooks and how he *never* takes anything but a Purple Door. So I got worried and thought I'd stolen somebody's trip and started to radio about it, and he started laughing and said he'd made it all up and really couldn't tell a Blue from a Purple Door.

You know what? She's a taxi driver.

Yep, she lies real good.

I'm not lying. That's the truth. And then there was the guy at Deep Cove and it was all dark and foggy out there early this morning . . .

Don't want to hear about it.

Well, how about the woman who was going to hit me if the car didn't stop rocking?

Why was the car rocking?

How should I know? Drivers who complain about the condition of the cars do not work for Purple Door, to quote our beloved manager. We were sitting at a red light, rocking, and she says I'm *so* nervous and if this car doesn't stop rocking, I'll hit you. So I says, lady, why don't you just yell at me instead, so she did. She was going to the police station because her husband assaulted her.

Yeah?

Yeah. Are you sure you wouldn't like to hear about Deep Cove?

You didn't get a fare in Deep Cove as well?

No, I took this guy there was all, and it was all foggy early this morning and not a soul around, you know . . .

Don't want to hear about it.

Are you sure? It was all dark and foggy . . .

I'm sure. He's sure. We're all sure.

Oh . . . Well, how about the drunk who fell down the stairs . . .

We've already heard about that one. And we don't want to hear about Deep Cove.

Frank Anchuk came to the window.

Anchuk! Do you want to hear about what happened in Deep Cove?

No. He slammed the window shut.

By that time they had all gone but George Amato. You had a good day then? he said.

Oh sure. Did you?

Not bad.

Does the traffic ever get you down? Shannon asked.

Does it! They levered me out once and took me to the psychiatric ward. I was stuck in this traffic jam at Woodwards and they had to come and take me away.

Are you kidding?

No, I was in the psychiatric ward.

But you're still driving cab?

What else is there to do?

Dunno. Sure was dark and foggy in Deep Cove.

At least there's no traffic there.

She was sometimes a personable person. Sometimes people called her beautiful and sometimes ugly, which goes to show she wasn't a proper woman since with proper women there is no doubt whether they are beautiful or ugly.

For a while, with the fervour of the early days of Women's Liberation, she tried to think of herself as a woman, but we meet her when all her dreams are dying. At this time, also, she was surprised to discover that it was more painful to acquire dreams than to lose them. She resolved there would be no more dreams and she thought of herself now as a broad or a bitch or some such name; hardly ever as a woman.

Other drivers had given up asking her out because she wasn't an easy lay and she was bored with evenings of heavy drinking. Passengers often asked her for a beer or a date, but less often than they assumed she was a whore. She found it difficult to distinguish between those who considered her a whore and those who saw her as a potential wife – the only two possible roles for women – and therefore refused all dates with passengers.

Once she broke the rule. Only once. But once too many. She drove a professor, newly-arrived, around the city while he found a place to live. It was a good fare and so she was grateful and friendly and even laughed once.

This was still the time Bradley was getting asked to university parties, and months later, at the first such party she had ever been to, she met the professor again and he remembered her, which blew her mind. He said he would call her and carefully noted her number, and she thought he didn't really count as a passenger since he hadn't asked her in the cab. But then nothing happened for a few weeks. Maybe he was sick or something. Having helped him find it, she knew where his apartment was, so she stopped by his place one afternoon with the cab. He was delighted to see her, overwhelming her with charm and expensive wine. She staggered back to the car in a daze and with a pain in her abdomen and drove around like that for a few weeks, but nothing more happened.

She took to driving by his place dozens of times a day, which was easy since he lived in the West End, and one morning she met him going out to his car. He was pleased to see her, since he thought it was an accidental meeting, and said he would call her soon. She asked when and he said soon. She said when. He said they would go out to dinner the following day. She was so nervous as to be ill, but he put her at ease and talked most charmingly and eruditely of all manner of things and ideas her passengers didn't even know existed. Then he took her home and screwed her several times most competently and held her in his arms in his sleep.

She staggered to work blissfully at 4 a.m. and three days passed in this daze of bliss. But two weeks went by and he didn't call. The screwing had increased her lust instead of abating it, so that the pain in her gut grew to almost unbearable proportions, and then she started bleeding so heavily there was no possibility of sex even if he did call.

She followed Bradley to another party. The professor was very late and had a dazed woman on his arm. Nevertheless, he was very pleased to see his old friend, the cabbie, again. He seemed, however, embarrassed by the fact that she was a cabbie, and told her she should go to university. He kept wandering off to talk to other women, and from the dazed looks on their faces, Shannon thought he must have laid half the women in the room in the months since he had arrived in town.

She asked him about this and his handsome brow furrowed and his charming manner grew charmingly sulky while he explained about *meaning* and *love*. He agreed with Women's Liberation and would not, therefore, insult any woman by making her his exclusive property. Shannon was confused, since she also believed in Women's Liberation and would have protested that wasn't exactly what it meant. But then he promised that she, ahead of all those other bewildered women, would be the one he would take home and screw that very night. She said no, which roused his masculine sense of challenge so that eventually, with great embarrassment, she explained she couldn't because of the pain and bleeding. She added, sullen now, that seeing him once a month was worse than not seeing him at all. He exclaimed in horror that she *must* be sleeping with others, not just him. It was the first time she had seen him upset. She thought about all the other men she could have slept with, and the image of a long line-up of erect penises formed in her brain. She explained to the professor that one couldn't sleep with passengers because they assumed she was a hooker, and he was amused and asked what was wrong with making money on the side. Shannon had quite a number of drinks and followed the professor around the room, telling him that he owed her thirty dollars and also asking if he knew where babies came from, and the professor was very pained by it all and was forced to leave the party early because of her hysteria. He did, however, pause long enough to pick up a more amiable woman to screw.

Shannon left the party too, and spent four hours walking home over endless miles of grey pavement. She didn't think anything and she didn't cry, she only walked and walked and walked through the night, conscious of nothing but the hollow sound of her footsteps and the strange sound of her breathing.

Bradley was sitting up, reading and drinking a beer, when she got home, but she didn't say anything to him, only went to have a shower and put on clean clothes and went to work.

For a long time Shannon was a new driver and then one day she was an old driver. She didn't know how it happened. She was sitting on the Blue stand and got a call for one of the envelope deliveries, and thought she had been driving cab for a long time already and nobody asked her any more what else she did, and if she thought about herself at all, the image included a car and a radio. She felt funny walking. Drivers look funny walking.

She didn't get lost very often any more and resented little old ladies giving her directions. She had favourite routes and resented passengers having their own preferences.

She knew all about the city and watched the traffic get gradually worse, pollution increase, monsters being built, and all the other changes. Long-haired entrepreneurs changed the ugliness of Water Street into the ugliness of Gastown, and now instead of old men begging, there were young men begging. The city never really changed; it had a way of transforming change like a great sprawling organism which absorbs foreignness into its own body.

The ugliness of the city was most obvious in the morning before the sun warmed up the muck. It was always cold in the morning. If she put on too many clothes on a spring morning, then it would be too hot later in the day and there was nowhere to put a jacket in the cab. Passengers even complained about the newspaper. They expected their servants not to have the cab or their minds cluttered up with a personal life.

Cold. Fog. On McGill, groups of Chinese women huddled on street corners waiting for the truck to come by. They made even less money than cab-drivers. On Water Street, a bunch of kids were sniffing glue from a plastic bag and one of them tried to run in front of the car, but Shannon cleverly swerved around him.

By the time she got to the yard, Bradley's car was warmed up. Out into the cold again, and into the Drivers' Room which was cold because the door wouldn't close. Night drivers dazedly made out their sheets, too tired to remember their social insurance number. Not too tired to make inane comments. Nobody mauled her any more. Eventually they would stop even making comments, as she never answered them. Sometimes she went to look at their sheets to find out what she could expect that day, but it was hard to tell from the night sheets whether or not it would be a good day.

Out into the dark again to find the cab. Being a spare driver meant it was always a different one, and she could hardly ever find it right away. Around and around the dark yard, avoiding the men wandering around for the same reason. If she told them which car she was looking for, they would keep an eye out for each other's cars and thus shorten everyone's search, but even if they asked her, Shannon didn't answer. Experience had taught her it was unwise. She had stopped smiling for the same reason. A smile on the part of a lower-class female person might lead to rape or a jail term for soliciting.

Finally in the cab, radio turned on, will the fucking thing start, should I check the tires? She never checked the tires and was occasionally pleased to find she had ripped the hell out of a tire by driving around with it almost flat. Most cars ran so badly it was hard to tell if the tire was flat. Book into town, not a soul around. A few hookers at Davie and Granville. Cold in the fashionable clothing. Not many. Pushers. Drunks. Nobody wanted a cab. Six in town by the Black Angus. All the drivers had moved here from the Skillett. Coffee to go. A few of the drivers yelled at her but she didn't reply. Back across the street to the cab, carrying the coffee. A drunk tried to stop her and she didn't push him but walked carefully around him. Safe in the cab. It's not safe walking. Morning streets are cold and violent. Women get beat up all the time. It's only illegal to beat up men, and it's illegal to kill women. So few men get jailed for rape that it can no longer be considered illegal.

At Denman and Nelson a pimp hailed the cab. Away, she said to the radio and it answered: roger. Now that she was an old driver already, she thought of all men in suits as pimps. This pimp spoke with an accent and told her he was a businessman from West Germany and that he was in Canada making deals. He liked Canada. The girls have nice body, he said. Would she have a drink with him. Shannon said no, and her voice sounded odd because usually she spoke only to the radio. The pimp thought it was a nice game and was very witty about why she should have a drink with him, but Shannon wasn't listening and only said no whenever he paused.

They had got to his address in south six before he looked at her and saw that she wasn't playing the game. It was amazing he noticed at all, as most of them didn't. Women were supposed to act in certain prescribed ways, and only rarely did men notice when they didn't, since they weren't looking for individual responses. The pimp told her again he was a businessman.

Two dollars and fifteen cents, Shannon replied. You fucking bitch, he yelled and Shannon cradled the mike in her hand, watching him carefully. I won't pay, you fucking bitch.

If I call on the radio, there will be ten burly drivers here in three minutes, Shannon said, caressing the mike button. He looked disbelievingly at her and got out of the cab. Shannon took a deep breath and got out her side, still holding the mike. I know where you're staying, she said, looking at him over the top of the car. He looked up and down the street and then, slightly purple, counted out the money. Shannon booked into south six and drove away.

She was first in six so she drove down to the B and G and sat there reading the paper and finishing her cold coffee. Nothing was happening on the hill but then not much was happening in town either. Finally she was sent to an apartment in Kits.

Five very drunk drunks got in the cab. She asked where they

wanted to go but they couldn't remember and then one of them realized she was a woman and practically clawed the back of the seat apart. Sweetheart, honey, you're so beautiful. Where ya wanna go, Shannon asked. It was going to be one of those days. The one sitting beside her gave her an address in the West End. We can take her upstairs for a drink, the drunk in the back said. The others said there wasn't anything to drink and they argued about that for a while, then asked her to take them to a bootlegger. Shannon said she didn't know any. They disbelieved her and argued about that to the West End. The one in the back kept saying she was beautiful and clawing the seat, and she told him to shut up, but he didn't hear her since that wasn't what he expected her to say. The one in front told him to shut up and the one in back replied that he wanted to get in her, it was a woman. It took them another five minutes to decide who was going to pay the fare, which was 95 cents.

She was 15th in town and fell asleep on the Rembrandt and missed a call, then moved down to the Davie and was 15th again. It was going to be a bad day.

A pervert with a suitcase whistled from the St. Helen's. Shannon motioned him to walk across the street since it was still early and there was little traffic. He motioned her to do a u-turn. She opened her window and hollered the cops would give her a ticket and she wasn't going to lose her licence for no pervert. But he wasn't walking across the street, and looked up and down for another cab. There were few cabs moving around because they had either fallen asleep or were reading the paper. The pervert finally gave up and walked across the street. He hurled his suitcase into the back seat angrily and sat in front. Hotel Vancouver, he said, but when she started driving he looked her over and said, no, the airport.

Going to work? Shannon asked.

No, I'm coming back from work. I'm from Saskatoon but I've been working up in McKenzie. I've spent three months there, and boy, I'm sure hard up for a woman. Do you have time?

Shannon stared at him while driving 50 mph over the Granville Street bridge. It always made them uncomfortable.

Well, he said, I have an hour before the plane leaves and I sure am hard up for a woman.

There's hookers all over Davie and Granville, Shannon said at last. I'm a cab-driver.

Oh, I wasn't meaning you were a hooker. I wouldn't pay for it. Shit . . .

A pig like you had better be prepared to pay, Shannon said, because you sure the hell will never get it for free.

Perverts are very sensitive. What did I do to you? he asked, hurt. Why are you insulting me?

You don't consider you insulted me?

No. Shit, no. I mean . . . You're a dame . . . And I'm not one of your ordinary construction workers, you know. I'm a *student*.

Shannon laughed. Everybody's a student.

Oh, are you a student? Geez, I'm sorry. I didn't mean to – I thought you were just another broad. Geez, I'm sorry. He looked at her with respect and talked ingratiatingly the rest of the way. At the airport he gave her $7.00 for a $5.50 trip and apologized once again. It was going to be a bad day.

Every morning is a new day. No matter how black and cold the early morning hours, it is a new day, as yet unsullied, untouched. Later, by the time the sun is up, it will have been irretrievably lost, messed up like every other day; gone to join the long file of unsatisfactory days which go to make up unsatisfactory lives. But now it was early morning, cold and black, and it was a whole brand new day as yet untouched.

Shannon drove around the West End, drinking coffee and singing. There were few people on the streets and the ones who were there were hurrying through the black and cold morning.

The first trip was some men from an apartment building. They hurried out, talking to each other in a language which sounded like Polish but wasn't. It turned out to be Yugoslavian. One had white hair and a white beard and the other was considerably younger. They gave her the name of a Yugoslav ship at Lapointe Pier and continued chattering to each other. English people don't talk to each other. People of almost any other culture chatter away for hours, giggling and sounding affectionate, but English people don't have anything to say unless they're drunk, when they don't have anything to say either, but persist in saying it.

The two men studied Shannon once in a while and discussed her in Yugoslavian. Finally the older of the two leaned over the front seat and cleared his throat.

I would like to ask you, he said, but I have not the courage. Shannon drank from her coffee and giggled. You want to know if I'm a boy or a girl, she said.

Yes. Precisely so. But I have not the courage. It is, perhaps, not a nice thing to ask?

No, it isn't nice. But I will reply, nevertheless. I'm a hippie.

A hippie?

Yes, and hippies don't come in sexes.

What is that, hippie? the man asked his younger companion.

That is children of the flower, the other explained.

Ah, yes.

You have them in Yugoslavia? Shannon asked.

Yes, some, I think.

Well, they're neither boys nor girls, are they? They come in entirely other groupings.

They were at Lapointe by that time, and Shannon needed instructions on how to find the ship, which the men gave her in respectful tones. Only when they were getting out did the old man refer to the previous subject.

You should come to Yugoslavia, he said. You would be much happier.

What would I do in Yugoslavia that would make me happier?

But he couldn't tell her because he didn't know which side of the sexual division of labour she was on.

The baby started walking quite late. Shannon worried about it without telling Evelyn, and supposed Evelyn was worrying without telling her. She also got a lot of colds and then one really bad bout of flu. Shannon could hear the baby coughing in the night, and worried about pneumonia and all manner of weird bacteria. One night when the coughing seemed particularly bad, she broke the pact of hostility and went upstairs before going to work at 3:30 a.m. Bradley, looking red-eyed and sleepless, was singing a revolutionary song to the baby. The baby had four teeth and smiled a lot between coughing spasms. After a suitable scrutiny, she allowed Shannon to pick her up. Holding the firm little body in her arms, Shannon realized with a shock that she was no longer holding a baby; she was holding a small girl who had a will of her own and daydreams and ideas.

I'm sorry, Bradley, she said. I won't be surly any more. Bradley nodded and awkwardly patted her head.

Evelyn was also relieved to put an end to the silence, but she thought cigarette smoke would irritate the baby's obviously fragile lungs and asked Shannon not to smoke upstairs. Shannon promised she wouldn't, but she was strung out and tired and couldn't go without a cigarette for very long, so her relationship with the baby continued to be an unsatisfactory one. She could only visit long enough to kitchy-koo once at the baby and get progress reports from Evelyn. Thus she didn't actually see the baby start walking, but only heard it.

The reason she didn't walk before, Evelyn said, is probably just that she's an awful coward. She's doing fine now except that standing up without something to grab for any length of time, like over one second, I mean, scares the hell out of her. I bought her some boots and they help her balance a lot.

Bradley was quite irritable about looking after her now. It's bad enough changing diapers, he said, but now she refuses to be fed. She has to have her hands in it, or a spoon, stirring and mushing it around, and it takes an hour to clean up after every meal. She doesn't sleep much in the afternoon any more, which doesn't leave me any time to myself.

Evelyn considered him an incompetent housewife and an inadequate mother. She also didn't approve of the songs he sang, so Bradley went to the Women's Liberation house to ask them about suitable songs, but they wouldn't let him in. He returned the next day carrying the baby, which he told them was a girl, and explained his wife had told him to come. The women in the house then let him in, served him coffee, and gave him the words to all the songs they knew, which were lamentably few.

Evelyn should have been pleased, but instead was angry at him for taking the baby out on a wet day. She was, in the meantime, having difficulties at her job, as she was late for work at least once a week. Finally the doctor told her politely that receptionists just couldn't be late all the time, and fired her. Evelyn was pleased at not having to work, though resentful about being fired. She told Bradley to get a job, since he wasn't a very good mother and let the baby get colds all the time.

Bradley couldn't get a job and brooded around the house, drinking a lot. Finally he went out of town on a construction job at Lornex Mines for eight weeks. He came home thin and irritable and swore he would rather starve than go to a concentration camp again. Both of them were getting unemployment insurance, however, so he didn't have to look for work immediately.

Evelyn hadn't proved to be much of a housekeeper either, as the old house was difficult to keep clean, and the baby still got colds. Between the two of them, however, they kept the house relatively free of dust and spent hours planning healthful meals for the baby. Neither of them had any time to themselves.

By then the baby had begun talking. She mostly said oh no! and oh dear! and she still laughed a lot. Now she could climb up and down stairs by herself and so could come and visit Shannon. Shannon nearly always slept after coming home from work in the afternoon, and she would awaken to find the baby sitting on her bed, poking a finger in her eye and exclaiming oh dear! oh dear! Eventually Evelyn persuaded her that Vitamin C was candy and she got fewer colds.

February 1971

A monotony of passengers get in and out of the cabs and the drivers are always tired and hardly ever remember any of their passengers. Fares all say the same thing, and after a while they all look the same. Only occasionally is anyone interesting enough to remember.

Shannon found that she remembered women passengers more often, although most passengers were men. Men all said the same thing in the same tone of voice and were only interested in whether or not she was married. In treating her like a robot, they became robotized themselves. Women came in different sizes and shapes, each with her individual problems.

Is this Skid Row? the woman asked, peering with dead eyes at the rain.

Yes.

Then I'm going home.

But she wouldn't have been there if she had a home to go to. She was a middle-aged Indian woman in a cheap print dress and sagging stockings. The man dropped her off at the New Empire Hotel, promised to call the next time he was in town, then went to the bus depot.

The next passengers were two young women from the West End. They told Shannon to stop in front of the Plaza Cafe, then one of the women got out and went into the cafe. A bit later she came out with a guy and they both walked towards Main Street, then disappeared into the rain. The other woman crouched in the back of the cab and locked all the doors. It was dark and pouring rain. People staggered in and out of the Plaza. A woman came and slammed on the window. Shannon opened the window.

This cab is taken, she said, but I'll call one for you.

Don wan no goddamn taxi, the woman said. She slammed on the window again and staggered away into the rain.

I hate this part of town, the woman in the back exclaimed. I'm always *so* frightened.

What did you come here for then?

The woman looked at her disbelievingly, sniffled, and leaned back into her corner. After about five minutes, she got upset again.

She's been mugged!

You're running up a lot of money on the meter.

Oh that! That doesn't matter. I'm just afraid something has happened to my friend.

Do you want to go and look for her?

No.

Would she run out on you?

No, no. She's my friend.

Another man and woman came and knocked on the window, and Shannon called for another cab which came immediately and took them away.

She's been mugged, the woman said. She's lying dead in that alley. She pointed out into the rain.

Want me to drive through the alley?

No. She's been killed. She was carrying $200.

Then the woman and the guy came back, looking very happy, and told Shannon they were all going back to Bute Street. But they were being followed by another car and got really agitated. Shannon tried to lose the car for them, but wasn't yet very good at it and kept stopping at red lights, to their chagrin. Finally, however, the car was lost. At Pender and Thurlow they asked her to pull into a parking lot, looking relieved and happy once again, when all of a sudden the car came towards them the wrong way on Thurlow. The guy threw the money at Shannon and they all ran. Shannon didn't wait to see what was going to happen but took off as fast as she could.

What were they doing? she asked Cliff Preston.

Buying heroin. You'll be driving people like that around about every second morning. You can always tell if they lock all the doors. They're either nervous or they've got some on them, maybe in their mouth in silver paper. If the cops come along, the locked doors give them time to swallow the stuff. If it happens to you, open the doors when the cop tells you, but do it slow.

You wouldn't turn in junkies?

Hell, no. I don't know anything. That's what you gotta do, not know anything. I guess I got more respect for junkies than for cops.

Where do they get so much money?

If they live in the West End, they're probably call girls. Women junkies nearly always pay for their habit with prostitution.

Or they take junk to stand it. Now I think about it, at various times men have complained to me about all the hookers being on junk. I guess it's like having pesticide in your meat. Christ.

Why do you drive a cab?

I was laid off my job after I was 40. Men over 40 can't get a decent job.

Oh yeah. Women. Indians.

Do you . . . It's a race and no matter how fast you run, you've already lost?

Yeah. Like that. We have as much chance of getting a decent job as flying to the moon.

But Apollo 12 was even then speeding moonward and there was definitely more chance of flying to the moon.

You can't work for Purple Door if you don't turn in higher sheets, Frank Anchuk had told her. Well, here was a good fare. Fat, middle-aged, with a crew cut, coming out of an apartment on Cambie carrying a paper bag. He had a drinker's red face. He wanted to be taken home to a West End apartment where he could shower and dress while Shannon waited, and then he was going to Burnaby. It was a good fare and came to $11, all of which Shannon wrote on the sheet because she was still a stupid driver. She called him Sir and he called her Doll, and she didn't complain because he was a good fare and she couldn't work for Purple Door if she didn't turn in higher sheets.

I phoned my lawyer, the man said, and my lawyer told me that if I murdered someone or robbed a bank he could get me off easy, but if I got an impaired driving charge there wasn't anything he could do about it.

He was a businessman and earned $24,000 to $30,000 a year and had 180 people working for him which, he said, proved anyone could get rich in this country. Shannon pointed out that what he had just proved was that the chances of getting rich were 180 to 1. She also told him the Status of Women report showed women earned an average of less than half of what men earned and that few women got to be heads of anything. He got very unhappy and said it was a stupid conversation, and then started telling her about a race horse he had bought for $4,500. Shannon made all the right comments and didn't tell him that was more than her year's income, because it was such a good fare.

One of the secrets of the ruling class, Shannon told Gerald, is that they don't usually spend any money. For example, I took a guy to the airport one day and he said if it was a penny more than $4.50 he would take the Airporter. It was more, of course, but I only charged him $4.50 since we had made a deal. Ordinary people would feel parasitic doing that as a routine. Then there was this teenage girl from one of those huge houses with a park around it in Shaughnessy. Carrying a long white dress in plastic, she was, and going to the Bayshore to attend a party being given for Jerry Wagonwheels and the Chariotracers. A teenage boy came running out to ask if she was going anywhere near Oak and 17th and I said it was the same difference to go that way, even though she didn't want him to come. He said irritably: C'mon, it won't cost any more, and the girl asked me again, although I had already said it wouldn't cost any more to go that way. She finally let him come along.

How's the baby? Gerald asked. Shannon hadn't yet succeeded in convincing him that an individual solution couldn't be found in dope and mysticism, and he didn't like hearing about social classes.

Oh, the baby. Shannon grinned all over. We're all kind of embarrassed because we thought she was slow. She is developing really fast, doing everything at once that she was supposed to do in stages, and she's had her hair cut which makes her look older. It was probably the colds that kept her sickly for so long. She is *very* pleased with her new appearance and preens herself in front of my mirror for hours at a time. Pretty, pretty, she croons, patting herself.

She's talking.

Oh yes. She's beginning to make sentences already, her favourite being Come *here*, Mommy. She spends a lot of time poring over books, chattering crazily and giggling over each page. She helps Evelyn with dusting, mopping, sweeping, and talks all the time, and she likes playing with the dishes in the sink. Her favourite expression right now is By *Jeeeesie*! and her favourite occupation is sticking small marshmallows in her belly button. Bradley taught her that and all sorts of other silly things. Right now he says Viva Ché all the time instead of Hello so the baby will think that's how you say hello. Dumb bastard. I try and counteract his bad influence, but she doesn't come and see me so much any more. I'm always tired. And she is hard to deal with. Evelyn says it's typical two-year-old characteristics. She gets really frustrated because she can't explain anything, and does all sorts of dumb things, then sits there waiting for you to do something. So I yell at her. Then I apologize. The kid is really confused. But I'm so fucking tired all the time. And Evelyn walks around feeling guilty. This baby has so many things other babies don't have and Evelyn feels guilty that she has too much. And then she thinks about what there is for her to grow up to. She's, you know, so sweet and joyful, and there isn't anything for her to grow up to. Evelyn says if she gets pregnant again she'll have an abortion. She says, Evelyn does, that it was all Bradley's fault, and that she never wanted to have anything to do with sex but he showed her in the marriage laws that she had to. She said that he was supposed to support her but I don't know if the marriage laws say anything about that. How's a kid supposed to grow up normal with parents like that? They think it's funny, and the baby sits around laughing all the time. Later on she'll probably disapprove of them, but now she just laughs all the time. But there isn't anything for her to grow up to.

The woman told Shannon she was going to VGH and apologized for carrying two suitcases, but she said that, in the psychiatric ward, people wore their own clothing so she needed a lot of stuff.

How-do-you-like-cab-driving, most people say in a mechanical fashion, because that's what you say to cab-drivers. But this woman asked: What sort of job is this? and Shannon looked at her in surprise because from her tone of voice it was obvious she wanted to know.

Shannon told her it was mostly a shitty job except for brief periods of exhilaration, and then looked at her again.

You look better than I feel, she said, why the psychiatric hospital?

I hate my job, the woman explained.

Oh. Can't you get another job?

No. I keep looking but there aren't any others. So I do it for as long as I can stand it and then I go to the psychiatric hospital for a while. I'm lucky. I don't need electric shock treatment because insulin works for me.

After that you can stand the job?

For a while. I teach ballet. I used to be a social worker but I was clever and ambitious and so I got promoted. I didn't want to be promoted, I only wanted to be clever and ambitious. That was when the trouble started. I liked being a social worker, but as a supervisor, I had a nervous breakdown. Supervisors can't go and get insulin treatment. Neither can uppity-ups who have nervous breakdowns go back to being ordinary social workers again.

So now you teach ballet and get insulin shock at regular intervals.

Yes. It's not . . . They said I would never make my own living but here I am, at 55, having been independent all my life.

You don't consider welfare an alternative?

No. No welfare. We'd have to give up the house then. My sister and I have a house and the taxes are rather high. I'm not sure that welfare would make us sell it, but certainly they wouldn't give us enough to pay for upkeep and taxes. No, I'll always make my own way.

You work at a job you hate to pay for insulin shock to make you stand the job?

It pays for a great deal more than that. The house. Pride. It would be a good job, if I didn't hate it. It keeps me in really fine physical condition. There are so few choices for women . . . Men have more . . . It seems . . .

Who said you wouldn't be independent?

Everybody. In my day, girls were supposed to be looked after. Nobody would marry me because we come from this really strange family, or a family everyone said was strange, and everybody said since nobody would marry me, I would have to be looked after in some institution. But I'm 55 and I've always been independent.

Well, that's something. Too bad you can't get another job.

There are so few choices for women. They've got you in a cage. If you're bad they tighten the bars around you so you've got no space at all. Then they give you back the original cage and call that freedom.

An elephant was reported on Granville Street one morning. A little later someone saw it on Smithe, and then on the bridge.

Is it pink?

Does it want a cab?

The despatcher told everyone to shut up about the elephant already. A little later 87 said from the Howe stand:

If there was 98 more, there'd be 101.

101 what?

Dalmatians.

Well, try not to look like a fire hydrant.

Are they pink?

Do they want a cab?

Don't take Dalmatians. They don't tip. Elephants, on the other hand, tend to be rather large tippers.

The kid from the Gulf of Georgia was going to south four, which made it a good trip on a slow morning. The kid was 20 and thought he was impossibly old, practically over the hill, and would never again in his life have any fun. Shannon looked him over and remembered the pain of being 20. She told him he would never be so old in his life again but, of course, he didn't believe her.

In the afternoon, she went to find a steady car. Bradley and Evelyn had made several payments on the furnace, and Shannon had paid off a small portion of the student loans, so they were no longer about to garnishee her wages.

Spare drivers got all the wrecks nobody else wanted to drive, and Shannon had had several minor accidents – one because the car wouldn't steer and another because the brakes pulled. She had been told, however, that drivers were not allowed to complain about the condition of their cars if they wanted to continue working, so she didn't complain any longer about the condition of her car. But she thought that, as a steady driver, she would be allowed to repair the car.

At the most recent meeting of the Safety Committee, she had not complained about the condition of the car and so had not got any points against her and was instead commended. Also, Jim Madison had told her to come and see him when she wanted a steady car. She found him lying under one of his cars in the garage, with another man talking to his feet. They were agreeing that anybody who didn't have a job was just too lazy to work.

Shannon said that wasn't so. She said everybody was too lazy to work when it came to that, but everybody worked because only people who had jobs were allowed to live without being driven mad. Jim climbed out from under the car and gave Shannon a lecture about laziness and unemployment.

Jim said the capitalist system was the best one because everybody was free. Shannon said they weren't free because everyone was forced to do stupid jobs. Jim said that was a good thing because if people weren't forced to work they wouldn't work. Shannon asked how then he could still maintain it was a free society, and he replied you couldn't have a free society because people were too lazy. He himself owned 23 cabs and worked 10 hours a day, 7 days a week. Shannon said that was less hours than most cab-drivers worked and they just barely made a living, while Jim was getting awful rich what with cheating the insurance and all. Jim said he didn't cheat, only claimed what was owing to him. Shannon asked why then didn't everyone else, and how come the poor weren't allowed to sleep at night? He said they were lazy. Anybody who wanted to could make it, and if they didn't, it was their own fault.

You're free to do what you want, he said. You can choose whatever you want to be. You can be a consumer or not a consumer. It's a free country and I can prove it. Look at me, I own 23 cabs and *I don't have a colour TV.*

Shannon stared at him for some time, and then said the only thing she could think of which was: why not? This irritated Jim and he said that proved it was a free country and that anybody could get a job.

It's a good thing you think so, Jim, Shannon said, because that's what I'm here about. A job. You need steady drivers?

No, he said and climbed back under the car. He never spoke to Shannon again.

That's two down the drain, Shannon told Gerald.

Who is the other one?

Giovanni. I turned in such low sheets he said I could never drive a car of his again.

It's all about sheets, is it?

Yeah, it's all about sheets. That's why you're out there, to make money for the owner. But turning in high sheets is really hard to do. There's only two kinds of guys who turn in high sheets. One kind is the determined, stable family man. These guys drive 6 or 7 days a week and are always on time and don't stop to eat or have coffee, and I know one guy who never goes to the bathroom the whole shift. They always look sick, these guys, and they suckhole the company, and I don't suppose they talk much and I suppose they just go home, eat and sleep, and then get up and go to work. Sometimes they take holidays. The other kind are the highballers. They're generally younger and they hustle like crazy. They very often have accidents because of their speed and jumping lights and stuff. They also do all sorts of prohibited things like picking up in suburban zones, booking into zones before they get there, answering for trips when they're not on a stand, clearing before the passengers are out of the car, and all that stuff. After work they drink themselves out of their minds and don't get much sleep and are simply terrible to get as passengers. Usually these kinds of guys get into a lot of accidents, but they're forgiven mostly because of their high sheets. Gerald, are you interested in all this stuff?

Sure.

I don't know why you should be. What are you reading?

James Joyce.

Christ. Are you eating right?

I got some yogurt.

That's good. Are you getting any protein? Meat and eggs and cheese and stuff.

Cheese.

Good. I think I'll try the company. Most of the cars are owned by different individuals, but the company has a few.

The man to see was Frank Anchuk. He was pleased to see Shannon leaning across the counter in the office, and told her she got better-looking every day. Shannon attempted to smile but she hadn't smiled for so long her face muscles had forgotten how to contract in the proper fashion. She asked Frank if the company needed a steady driver. He said they didn't right then but there was a guy leaving soon. Shannon asked how soon.

Frank asked why she didn't comb her hair. Shannon said she didn't like combing her hair and it didn't comb very well anyhow.

Even if I don't comb my hair, I'm better looking than you are, she told Frank.

And another thing, he said, I don't want you talking politics to the passengers. I've mentioned that to you before.

Look, the passengers love me. I'm charming and whatever I say, they love me. I bet you get people phoning you to tell you what a nice person I am.

He looked embarrassed.

I didn't say you weren't charming, he said. I just don't want you talking politics to the passengers.

You've been saying that ever since the War Measures Act. The War Measures Act didn't say I couldn't talk politics to passengers. Whenever something like that happens, there are people like you falling all over themselves to exceed the repression. You know in Germany, the psychiatrists started killing the mentally ill because they thought Hitler would like it. After, they pleaded orders, but there were no orders.

I was in the war, young lady! You can't tell me anything about the war.

I wasn't talking about the war, I was talking about fascism. You gonna let me drive a company car or not?

Why don't you buy a blue jacket?

What?

You'd look nice in a blue jacket.

I look nice in a red jacket. This red jacket is one I bought at the Army and Navy for $8. They didn't have any blue jackets for $8. Angela Davis is a Communist and she doesn't wear a red jacket. The War Measures Act didn't say people couldn't wear red jackets. Don't be so paranoid.

Well, just don't talk politics to passengers.

What if they start the conversation?

Then you just agree with whatever they say.

That's politics. You gonna let me drive a company car or not?

Well, like I said, we don't need a driver right now. But why don't you come into my office and we'll talk about it. He leaned across the counter, ugliness and violence on his face, and from previous experience Shannon knew this was the sexual look for men.

Go fuck yourself, she said.

None of the one-car owners needed drivers. Shannon thought she might as well stay as a spare driver a while longer. She didn't tell Evelyn about it all because Evelyn would have pointed out, quite correctly, that it was almost as bad as looking for a job except you didn't have to wear nylon stockings.

In the spring of 1971 there was a massive anti-war demonstration in Washington. Demonstrators were determined to bring business to a complete halt but they failed to do so. Many, including Dr. Spock, were jailed but there were too many to prosecute properly.

The war went on as before.

In June, the exposés of the secret Senate reports appeared in the New York *Times*. They had been provided to the newspaper by Daniel Ellsberg, a former Defense Department aide. These reports of U.S. involvement in the war in Vietnam up to 1968 included information about U.S. plans to make war against North Vietnam even before the 1964 Tonkin Gulf incident, covert commitment of U.S. ground combat troops, and attempts to keep escalation of the war a secret. The U.S. government obtained court orders to stop publication of the stories in the New York *Times* and Washington *Post*, but other papers continued printing the exposés. Several reporters and Daniel Ellsberg were jailed.

The war went on as before.

The anti-war movement, which had been disintegrating, pretty well disappeared completely. Dope, religion, and other individual solutions to despair claimed a larger number of people.

The cracks which had begun to appear years before became larger and engulfed the American dream. But instead of revolution, Americans leaned towards fascism. Ideally, in a situation where the ruling class has either lost its power or gone berserk, another class should seize power, but the American ruling class was still too powerful to be defeated and the people too little aware of their power to organize themselves properly. Thus the Black Panthers died and the anti-war movement disintegrated into dope and jesus. The back-to-the-land movement gained a large number of adherents in spite of the razed land of Vietnam.

Individual survival became more difficult in the gradually encroaching chaos and violence. Murderers, rapists and dope-dealers went unpunished but political offenders and the poor had the entire weight of the monolithic state thrown at them. People did not blame the berserk ruling class; rather, they identified with it, and saw themselves in support of, and even in control of, the increasingly mad actions. This was easily done by blaming some group other than the ruling class for the chaos. Black Panthers were shot, to "restore law and order," and protests were minimal. The rising crime rate was blamed on people other than white people and this was accepted. Sexual deviation and rape became more prevalent and women became more definitely an "other"; a hostile group to be beaten into submission. A whole new category to hate was created and named hippies, and parents turned against their own children and named them responsible for the chaos. The children, having been detached, developed a whole philosophy of detachment.

In Canada, the hippies incorporated the American philosophy in its entirety except for the racism of the counterculture. The decent citizenry became more racist, and sexism increased. Women's Liberation talked about winning all sorts of things, but in fact was only carrying out a holding action against the increasing sexism of the society.

In Vancouver, there was going to be a hotel built at the entrance to Stanley Park. Various hippie groups had previously talked about making Stanley Park into a people's park as in San Francisco, but this failed because it always had been a people's park. Only now there was going to be this huge hotel at the entrance. A plebiscite was held on the matter and over half the property owners in the West End voted for the hotel.

A group of communist hippies decided to occupy the property and physically prevent the hotel from being built. These were enlightened hippies so they were doing it for political reasons and would not allow the unemployed and others who had nowhere to go to park there. They poured scorn on the merely unemployed and went after the decent citizenry's good will by acting like good citizens, albeit with long hair. Unfortunately decent citizens didn't differentiate between good hippies and bad hippies, good communists and bad communists, so they didn't actively support the action in any case.

Only a few weeks after the enthusiastic and victorious occupation, Shannon, driving by the site, found it was deserted. This depressed her no end. Later in the summer, however, the unemployed moved in, set up tents and buses on top of the dying gardens and unfinished playgrounds, and dozens of people crashed there the whole summer and some until the following spring.

The same spring, a group of mothers from Raymur Place stopped the trains which were daily threatening their children's lives. They camped on the tracks at Pender and Raymur for a few days, and eventually a walkway was built. These women had previously been beaten down by welfare and marriage and capitalism, but this action got them out of despair and isolation and they began to plan other collective actions including a food coop. Unfortunately, they had also attracted the attention of the politically conscious and no fewer than eight Opportunities For Youth projects descended on them in the summer. These people considered for some reason that their pushing and prying and directing of people's lives was different from the government's doing the same thing.

Bradley walked with thousands in the May Day march and

came home filled with enthusiasm. Evelyn said it sounded like fun, but what was going to come of it? Nothing came of it.

Hearing the Indochinese women speak was a slightly different kind of experience for Bradley. Neither Shannon nor Evelyn had gone, and he woke both of them up to tell them about the Indochinese women. The three of them talked for several hours and decided that they should help the Vietnamese and that they should put their own lives together better, but they didn't know how to do either one.

Still in the spring, Shannon went to buy more 222s for her abdominal pain, and found some scruffy looking women in front of the drugstore. They were asking people not to shop at Cunninghams, but most people were going in anyway.

Are you Cunninghams' employees? Shannon asked one of the women.

No. Cunninghams isn't on strike, but Cunningham owns a warehouse named Hosken. Hosken employees have been on strike for over a year. We're doing a secondary picket to make the company negotiate.

Oh, you're Hosken employees.

No. It's illegal for them to do a secondary picket, so we're doing it for them.

You mean you're a whole different bunch walking around in the rain on behalf of somebody else?

Yes and we're going to organize women into unions and get more wages and better working conditions. Most Women's Liberation groups want to make women into executives and managers, but that still leaves most women typing and waiting on tables. They shouldn't just pay the minimum wage because they're women's jobs.

Amazing, Shannon said.

What do you do?

I drive a cab. See, there's my cab over there.

Far out!!! Why don't you come to our meetings?

Because I'm tired, Shannon said. And if you think it's far out to be a cab-driver, you're just the same as everyone else.

Oh, I thought it would be a neat job.

Well, now you know. Evelyn might come to meetings if the baby gets over this cold and doesn't immediately get another one.

Most mothers have those kind of problems.

And we live in this old house, and she keeps worrying that the roof will cave in. Evelyn would talk to me if she was able to cope, you know. We've been friends for a long time and she *would* talk to me, only the baby gets colds and Evelyn thinks the roof might cave in. Otherwise, she would talk to me.

Yes, I'm quite sure she would, the woman said kindly.

June 1971

Summer came soft and warm and all the spring flowers died. The sun rose early so that by the time Shannon had done her first trip, the first rays were filtering down through the muck above the city.

One morning when Shannon woke up, it occurred to her that she was a stuffed doll with tattered covering and with most of her stuffing hanging out. One of the night drivers had been robbed and beaten, but Shannon didn't worry about it because you can't hurt a stuffed doll. This knowledge also protected her from the constant fear of car accidents. She was pleased to find her first trip would take her to the airport. They made good coffee at the airport so she drove back slowly over the bridge, sipping the coffee and watching the morning sun come over the mountains. The day hadn't got messed up yet.

Later in the morning, she stopped to see a demonstration in front of the U.S. consulate. There had ever been only one good demonstration, which was when people marched into Blaine following the U.S. invasion of Cambodia. This morning's demonstration was the more usual variety.

The organizers had decreed it should be peaceful. One group disagreed and marched down Georgia and back again. When they came back, the organizers, who were Trotskyists, ran to line up at the door with the cops. Seven cops and twelve Trotskyists lined up military-style to protect the U.S. consulate from marauding hordes, which seemed counter to the spirit of anti-war demonstrations.

Withdraw U.S. troops now, yelled the Trotskyists, flashing the V sign for peace.

Smash capitalism, countered the Vancouver Liberation Front, waving their fists.

End Canadian complicity, shouted the Trotskyists with the V.

Power to the people, retorted VLF, clenching their fists. Nothing more seemed about to happen, and the whole thing seemed absurdly removed from the intention, which presumably had been to support the Vietnamese.

Shannon went to look for fares and found a crippled Portuguese man at the Austin. He told her that people should be given six months to get a job and if they didn't get one in the time allotted, they should be put in concentration camps. Shannon told him the upkeep of such camps was expensive and it would be easier to just give people $90 a month welfare and let them walk around the streets all night. They died just as fast that way.

The Portuguese man had come to Canada in 1955 and worked as a farm labourer. He worked 16 hours a day except Sunday, which he was given off. He was paid $55 and given a place to sleep. He was also supposed to get food, but he didn't know that and so paid for food out of his $55. After this he found there were better jobs to be had, and worked at some reasonably well-paid industrial job where he was crippled. Thus he had been well trained in hatred, as is necessary for a loyal citizen of capitalist society, and he limped around spewing hatred like vomit onto the streets.

The next passenger was a very drunk woman with a Halifax accent who tried to pay an 85 cent fare with $5. Shannon insisted she take $4 in change and she finally did. Shannon supposed she would only drink up the money anyway and swore to herself that next time she would keep all the money drunks gave her, as her fellow cabbies claimed they did. She also swore that beggars were getting no more of her change, but a huge man in front of the West told her he was hungry, so she gave him $2.

Back in the Drivers' Room, Anchuk opened a slot on the window with a slam.

You look like a hippie boy, he told Shannon, and Purple Door doesn't hire hippie boys.

I'm sorry, she said, I guess it's the way I walk or something.

It's your hair.

Oh.

It's your hair that makes you look like a hippie boy. Purple Door doesn't hire hippie boys, you know.

I'm sorry, she said again.

You look like a hippie boy. He slammed the window shut and then opened it again. And another thing. Those demonstrations. What do you know about war? You don't even know what you're talking about.

Do you?

Yes, I know. I was in the war. If it wasn't for me you kids wouldn't even be here.

If it wasn't for you there'd never have been a war.

He slammed the window shut and didn't come back.

Any possibility of someone killing him? Shannon asked the driver next to her.

Oh yeah, he's been beat up once already. But he's like that. Can't learn.

I want to be there when he's dying, Shannon said.

Oh, he's not such a bad manager. There have been worse.

Is it possible? Why don't we form a union?

This company has sure gone downhill. You know why?

Because of Anchuk.

He's done some good stuff. It's them Hindoos and Chinese who are coming in here wrecking it.

Wrecking what?

They keep hiring more and more of them. Soon they'll be running the place.

I can't stand racists. That's why drivers get screwed. Because

they're stupid. You think it's the fault of immigrants, for chris-
sake, when they're in the same powerless position you are.
I can't stand the bastards.
I don't suppose they like you much either.

July 1971
When there is a slight wind on a summer morning, the smog
gets blown away and the mountains sparkle clear and blue above
the city. On the shaded streets, trees keep away the heat, but
there are none of these in the east end of the city.

Shannon's favourite streets were Elliott, Blenheim, 16th Avenue, and best of all, one short block of 14th between Maple and
Cypress, where big old trees hung over the street. In the east
end, there was just the grey shimmering heat from the pavement. In the morning before the sun came up, Chinese women
sat in groups on the grey pavement, some with stools, all with
big hats, waiting for the trucks. The trucks were old and broken-
down and rough. They only paused for a short time at each
corner, while the women quickly climbed on the back and either
squatted or sat on their little stools, resting. It would be a long
hot day on the farms and it paid very little. They got paid as
much as domestic labourers, who got paid less than taxi drivers.

Early in the morning, Shannon drove some people looking for
heroin and then she got a trip to the airport. The timing was just
right and when she drove slowly back over the bridge, the sun
was just coming up and everything was painted orange. She
picked up a flag in south six and took him downtown, and it was
such a beautiful morning she went for breakfast with him.

He was studying to be an electrician at BCIT. He had been in
nurse's training at the Royal Columbian, but was thrown out
halfway through his training though he was getting the highest
marks in the class. They told him men didn't fit well into nurs-

ing because they weren't "yielding and pliable." He had then made an unsuccessful suicide attempt. He told all this to Shannon breathlessly, knowing she couldn't sit there for very long listening to him, but he had to tell someone.

The rest of the day, passengers told her it was a nice day and asked her if she was a boy or girl. If she told them she was a boy they got mad, indicating they only asked the question as a put-down and knew all along she was a girl. Then they asked if she was married. She had long since refused to answer that question. Sometimes she told people she wouldn't answer because it wasn't any of their business and they only asked because they couldn't pigeon-hole her without knowing about her marital status. Women are defined by the men they live with, or are defined by the fact that they couldn't find a man to live with, and Shannon explained they must judge her simply by what they saw. Most often, however, she simply ignored the question. Similarly with the boy or girl question, there were times she thought it was funny to answer non-committally, like saying yes, or, are you trying to start something, Mac? Most often she just didn't reply, or grunted.

The other part of the series of questions fares ask cab-drivers are about the Experiences. You must have many Experiences, they say, licking their lips in anticipation, you must be bothered a lot by rough passengers. Not so much as I'm bothered by people asking about it, Shannon had once replied, but you don't get tips that way. Sometimes she thought people were actually being sympathetic, and told them about traffic problems and the constant possibility of car accidents, but they didn't want to hear about car accidents, only about rape and decapitation and titillating items like that.

She went to see Gerald, who was then living in some dumpy room he rented by the week. He ate one week and walked around all night, and the next week he rented a place to sleep and didn't eat. Welfare didn't provide enough for both rent and food. He had a beautiful face. There had been times when Shannon wanted to touch him, reach out to him, but she no longer did. He seemed perfect as he was, complete and unreachable in his alienation.

Did you finish James Joyce? she asked.

Yes.

What was it about?

Life. Now I'm reading Herman Hesse.

Christ. Have you still got some yogurt?

Yes.

Well, I brought some brewer's yeast.

You think I need vitamins more than poetry?

Of course. Everybody does. Well, they need both, but vitamins first. I also brought you a hamburger. With cheese.

What's wrong with you?

I'm happy.

Why?

I don't know. This morning I got up before the sun and the birds were singing their acid rock to the sky and it was a whole new morning. Most mornings in the city are filled with drunkenness and despair, but summer has arrived. I always go stupid in the summer. All things seem possible in the summer. Before the sun came up, when I was driving the early morning dope seekers, there was a kid in a purple shirt riding a bike in circles on the Granville bridge, shouting at the mountains and singing to the sky. He waved when I drove by, and I saw that he was filled with joy so intense it was spilling in waves over the bridge and into the city, so that when I got to Davie, I wasn't surprised to see four kids dancing on Granville, and farther on, two boys leaping over parking meters, just before the sun came up.

Did they find any heroin?

Who?

Didn't you say you were driving junkies?

Oh yeah. At the Chick and Bull. They didn't like going there but couldn't find anywhere else. I don't know why they couldn't, because it's really easy to buy dope. It was a good trip. Right after, I went to the airport and then picked up a flag in south six of all places. A kid going to BCIT.

Why don't you go back to university?

I had a passion for knowing and discovered it isn't possible to know, only to believe. But I was brought up right, being poor, and the requirements of the days have caused me to transcend nihilism, despair, and even incipient alcoholism. Too bad about you, coming from a rich family, there isn't any hope.

Gerald accepted his fate without protest. I suppose next you're going to tell me about the baby, he said.

Oh yeah, the baby. She's so marvellous. She's talking better every day and making grammatical sentences and everything. She spends hours scribbling on paper and now she's started to draw on the walls. She doesn't like being helped with her clothes and Evelyn says it takes three hours to dress her. Evelyn complains about not having any time to herself, but she's so patient all the time. I don't know how she does it. The baby gives me these harangues in the afternoon when I'm so tired I can hardly see, and I tell her to go away but she talks. It sounds good, legitimate words interspersed with gibberish so it sounds like a speech. She acts so self-righteous when she's doing that. And then turns shy. Evelyn's sister was visiting and the baby took an immediate dislike to her and wouldn't talk or play or anything, just stood around sucking her thumb and saying NO to everything. Nasty child. Evelyn banished her to the basement a few times when she was bad, but she doesn't do it anymore, and even apologized when I said the baby would start to think of me or my life as punishment.

July 1971

The birds were doing their things as usual in the morning, but the sun was up before Shannon. The office yelled at her for being late. Her first passengers got in at the Davie stand and told her to go around various back streets to avoid the cops who were riding up and down Granville. After she had delivered them to the Plaza, they complained about the fare. The guy had just enough money to buy dope if he didn't pay the fare. After some haggling, the woman paid.

Shannon drove around for a while. It was a sleepy summer morning. She found a flag who wanted to go to the Austin. Back on the Davie stand, she got the bartender from the West Hotel who was going to stack beer or something.

Hot, he said. Helluva place to work. You throw them out one door and they come crawling in the other.

After which, she sat on the Columbia stand reading the paper. The guy who got in looked like all the other ones: dirty, unshaven, drunk, bloodshot. But then Shannon remembered his eyes.

Haney? she said.

Right. Christ, my head hurts.

Shannon told the despatcher she was away and that she didn't need him, having found her own fares all morning.

The man was fat and old and bald and drunk, with nasty blue eyes. The only nice thing about him was his hands, which were calloused, with broken and dirty fingernails. He owned a store in Haney, and this time he had come to Vancouver because there was no longer quite enough business to cover expenses. After a few drinks he'd felt richer than hell, but now he was beginning to be poor again. When they were on the Lougheed he said:

It hasn't changed, at least I haven't noticed the difference.

What?

The world. You told me you were going to change it.

Oh. Yeah. That was a long time ago. There is no hope.

None?

None.

Did it take you all these years to learn that?

I guess I'm pretty dumb. You're supposed to learn that on your first job so that you no longer trouble capitalism with incipient rebellion.

They should teach you that at university.

They don't teach you anything at university.

Why do people go?

Dunno. I suppose they think degrees might be useful.

What for?

Lots of things. Like, for instance, the morning sun is now shining in my eyes because the sun visor on this car won't swing around to the side. If I had a degree I could hang it right here to keep the sun out. Or if I had a degree in psychology I could show it to my fares and they would be more successfully intimidated. Think they'd mind?

Nope. They'd probably give you bigger tips.

Only a few short years ago, I was out to save the world, and now I've been reduced to foraging for dimes.

You know what? You're insane.

Quite, Shannon said proudly. Do you mind?

No, I'm delighted. It's not often you see insanity unashamed, walking down the street.

I'm not walking, as you see. I'm driving. This car has no shock absorbers or whatever it is a car is supposed to have to glide you smoothly over bumps, so you better tell me when we're about to hit a bump.

It's okay, the man said. If I bounce up and mash my skull I can sue the company for a million dollars and we'll split the take.

Do you think they would pay a million dollars for your head? Shannon asked doubtfully.

You're right, they wouldn't. If I had a degree, my head might be worth a million. Yes, I can see it would be useful.

It's just a game. They don't teach you anything, and degrees are no longer useful because there are too many of them. It's just a game. It keeps up the illusion of civilization and progress and all that. Women and Indians can't afford to go, and if they went, the only kind of jobs they could get are the same kind of shitty jobs they would get without a degree. It's a game. They teach you to be cynical, is all. Helps people accept racism and sexism as not only necessary, but amusing.

At Haney, Shannon waited in front of his house while he shaved and changed into clean clothing, then took him to his store. He looked a bit better when he came out, but was still mostly a fat and old drunk. At the store, he gave Shannon thirty cents and told her to get some coffee. The meter was still running. She walked down to the next block, to a small cafe which opened at six, and remembered that he took his coffee black.

Sit down for a while, he told her when she got back, I just have to get things straightened out here.

Shannon assumed he wanted something delivered or wanted to go home again, so she stood around drinking coffee and looking at the mountains.

D'you know what, she yelled at him. It's the most beautiful morning in the world.

How do you know? You haven't seen them all.

Maybe there are no others.

There must be, he said, wiping his hands on a rag. Every morning I get up at 4:30 and there are sure a lot of them.

Why at 4:30?

I feel bad at 4:30 so I get up. The hour of the wolf.

So what do you think about then?

Well, for the first while I think about all the people I owe money to, and that takes until about 5. Then I think about the people who owe me money, and that takes a considerably shorter period of time, so about 5:10 I start thinking about all the dirty rotten things I've done, and that's when I really feel bad. But then I start thinking about the dirty rotten things people have done to me, and I conclude I am not such a rotten bastard after all, and by about 6:30, I leave the house happier'n hell.

They both laughed and then he asked Shannon why she didn't sit down.

I sit in the taxi all day.

Relax. I'll only be a few more minutes.

When they tell you to relax, it's time to leave. I was relaxed, Shannon said, but now you've told me three times to be at ease, I'm getting rather tense.

Well, don't. My clerk will be here soon and we can go.

Go where?

Dunno. Down to the river or something.

What for?

Talk. I'm lonely.

I'm working, Shannon said.

So? I'm paying you for working.

He got out enough money from the cash register to pay the fare, and then another $6 for the nearly one hour of waiting time so far. See, he said, you don't have to worry about the money.

I wasn't worried about the money.

You should. Everyone has to make a living.

Not like this.

Like how? I want you to drive me down to the river, and your job is to drive the fare where he wants.

I don't gotta drive people anywhere I don't want to go.

Please?

A customer drove up and the fat old man went to carry some boxes out for him. Hey, come and see, he called. She went and saw that the customer had a whole bunch of rabbits in the back of his pickup. Takin' them to the auction, he explained.

You know what? Shannon said when he had gone. Brown rabbits have brown eyes and white rabbits have pink eyes.

They do not. All rabbits have pink eyes.

Brown rabbits got brown eyes.

You sure?

Yup. Brown rabbits got brown eyes.

He found the $6 Shannon had left on the counter and then got another $6 from the cash register to give her for another hour. All that money. So what the hell if he wanted to drive by the river and talk. Shannon threw the money back on the counter and then they argued about it for 15 minutes, at the end of which time he had put the bills in her red jacket pocket. It would be cool and green by the river.

What do you want? Shannon asked, slouching in the doorway. Men. You never say what you want. Down to the river to talk because you're lonely. That's what they all say. They all want to talk because they're lonely. Only they haven't anything to say and there's nothing I can say they want to hear. Why don't you say what you want so I'll know what I'm accepting or rejecting?

I told you. I don't have to be back here until 10 and it's a beautiful morning.

Shannon laughed. Would you want the cabbie to take you down to the river if he was a fat old man?

Sure. Why not? I get lonely. Fat, old man. Sure. Though I must admit skinny girls are more interesting. Please? I'm paying you for the time.

It would be cool and green by the river. Another step closer. It was always like that. They paved your way with promises of beauty, and in the end there was nothing but blood and pain and people screaming.

Fuck off, Shannon said. You bastards think relationships between people have to do with money. Stuff it. If you just wanted someone as insane as you are to talk to, why didn't you just ask me to drive down here after work?

Would you drive down here after work?

Are you crazy? All the way out here after driving all day? She handed him back the second $6 and walked to the car.

You won't change your mind?

No. Drop dead. She put the car in gear, then paused. Hey, don't I even get a tip for entertainment? He threw a $2 bill at her which landed on the seat as she drove away.

She didn't get many fares after that. It was impossibly hot and none of the taxi stands seemed to be in the shade. It would have been cool and green by the river.

But it was such a long road and a terrible price to pay for a bit of greenery. Someone had once promised a woman love and greenery, and now she lay in the gutter on the Columbia stand and wanted to die. The women who were once promised beauty and comfort now only wanted heroin. A little girl, raised to be cute, was raped and murdered for her prettiness. A nurse, promised honour and beauty, was dead with a knife in her back. They promised a pedestal for women but there was only work and fear and blood and death.

Not yet. Tomorrow. Next week. Next month. Put everything off until the next day; the odds are fairly high there won't be one.

It would have been cool and green by the river. Shannon thought about the river until it seemed the river was running through her brain. Nobody else. Not even the rabbits. Just the river, cool and green. All the fares complained about the heat, and Shannon agreed it was unbearable, smiling smugly and not letting on about the river.

July 1971

Blood. Why did there have to be so much blood? Summer Sunday morning. The cops were already there so there was nothing to be done. Maybe there's a war on. They won a round this morning. You aren't allowed to kill people with a gun or a knife. With a car, it's okay.

At 4:30 Shannon got a flag from the Lion's Tale which went to zone four, a bad place to end up on a Sunday morning. Nothing was happening anywhere else either, so she parked at Broadway and Commercial and fell asleep.

When she woke up, there was a man hobbling down Broadway shouting and waving. She drove towards him and he got in, explaining that his toe had been half cut off. She thought he was going to a hospital, but it turned out the toe had been hurt some days before and was already suitably bandaged, only he wasn't supposed to walk on it. He was going to Inlet Drive, which was a good trip, and he looked poor so Shannon didn't turn on the meter until they were almost at Boundary Road.

It all started when he lost his job. He got very drunk as a result of being laid off, and went to visit his fiancée. Her father refused him entry to the house because of his drunken state. So he got even drunker and ended up in Stanley Park. There he saw a cop at whom he thumbed his nose, though he knew it wasn't legal to thumb his nose at cops. The cop started chasing him. While running away, he stepped on a broken neon light and cut his toe half off. Following the night in jail and a visit to the hospital, he arrived home to find his landlady had evicted him because he was unemployed. There he was on the sidewalk, TV, cut toe and all. The guys across the road offered him a place to sleep and to keep his furniture and he accepted, but they were having a party with dope and stuff, and he and his TV both got bashed around. He wanted to leave, only they kept saying he would squeal to the cops and kept knocking him down. He had finally got away after being chased down 8th Avenue, and this was where, in his crisis-strewn life, Shannon had met him.

He assured Shannon she had saved his life by sleeping at Commercial and Broadway on a Sunday morning. Shannon was not loath to take credit for saving someone's life, but she hadn't seen anyone chasing him. She also didn't see the point of wrecking the TV.

She drove all the way back to Carrall and Hastings before finding another fare.

Where am I? the man asked.

Carrall and Hastings.

What am I doing here?

I don't know.

He thought about it for a while. Oh, he said, I remember, I was chasing women.

Did you catch any?

I don't remember. Married 22 years. She's fat and ugly like me, and she's been playing around with this 21-year-old. Well, two can play the game. Married 22 years.

Anyone would get bored sleeping with the same man that long.

But for five years! And I just found out about it. What would an old woman see in a 16-year-old?

Get em young, Shannon said, and then you can train em right. Men should be yielding and pliable.

What???

Train em young.

Are you married?

That's my business.

You're not a proper woman.

Maybe you're not a proper man and that's why your wife is playing around.

Oh God, I'm sick, the man moaned, holding his head.

Shannon felt sorry for him and patted his shoulder. Tell your wife you caught a woman even if you don't. She'll probably be pleased.

Oh God, he moaned.

Later in the day the transmission packed up, so she had to call for a tow truck. They gave her another car, which meant driving 12 hours since it was a late car. It was also difficult to steer and the horn blew every time she signalled to turn left.

She stopped in to give Gerald $20, and he asked her how come she could do that after what she had to do to earn it. She said it didn't matter and that he would pay her back eventually. Her gut ached and her back ached. Gerald needed new shoes.

After that she got a man and a woman from St. Paul's Hospital. The man kept arranging the woman's hair in a detached fashion and looking at her as if he was a farmer with a cow which could win prizes if carefully groomed. After they got out in south four, Shannon remembered where she had seen him before. She had driven him from zone seven to the Columbia once. He was a pimp with two women at the time, and thought Shannon should be the third. She called him every name she could think of, but he just sat back laughing. He told her she was responsible for child molesting. He thought that if men had an adult woman to practice perversions on, they would not kill children. Shannon said if a girl was only meat, it was better she died young. In any case, encouraging perversions caused more of them.

Shannon remembered how the man had pulled out a huge roll of $20 bills, and thumbed slowly through them, watching her face, before he found a $2 bill with which to pay the fare. She had remembered the roll of $20s much longer than she remembered his opaque fish eyes.

Shannon had forgotten to book into south four and the despatcher was calling for a car. She answered and he gave her an address and told her to go in and help, as it was a blind man. Shannon guided the man out to the car most carefully before she realized he wasn't blind.

I am a nervous breakdown, he said. Yesterday I am an ambulance. Which more or less explained everything. He also told her with considerable agitation that someone had tried to steal one of his three cars the night before and wasn't that a rotten thing to do to a sick man. Shannon said he didn't need three cars so it didn't matter if one got stolen, which upset him a great deal.

He wasn't going far, but at the house he asked Shannon to take him around the back because he was afraid. She did, holding his arm. He stank of liquor and fear and lust and a hundred unwashed days. A woman wordlessly opened the back door for him while he stood fearfully on the steps, clutching Shannon's arm.

When he had gone inside, Shannon thought how terrible it must be to be afraid on a sunny Sunday afternoon. Then she remembered the roll of bills and, walking back to the car, she saw a tormented tree crouched in one corner of the yard, and she saw also that the grass just barely covered the treacherous earth waiting to swallow her up.

She fled into four and then into five, where she finally got a delivery trip, one of the mysterious brown envelopes. Inside her head, the river which had been cool and green ran red with blood.

Isn't this an unusual job for a girl? the man from the Grosvenor asked.

What's usual? Waiting around to be screwed?

Oh, he said with acute embarrassment, you're women's lib.

Liberation, she growled.

She had been reading a National Geographic article on Kuwait, so to get the man over his embarrassment, she asked him if he did a lot of travelling. He said he did: Canada, Africa, the Middle East. That sounded like oil.

Have you ever been to Kuwait?

Yes, he said. It's uninhabitable except for the Arabs.

But this National Geographic says there are more foreigners there than citizens.

That would be since the 1950s when oil was found. They're rich now. I believe the per capita income is the highest in the world.

What does that mean? It could mean that one man gets a million dollars and a dozen others get nothing. Are there poor people?

Oh yes, but they are well looked after. The sheik spends an awful lot of money on them.

Who owns all the oil?

The sheik does.

And then he gives some of the money to the people?

Yes.

Does he have to?

No, but he's a very nice man.

How did he get to own all the oil? Why don't the people own any of the oil?

I don't know. Traditional, I suppose. There will always be those who have more and those who have less, human nature being what it is.

What is that? Shannon asked.

Come on! he said irritably.

I'm serious. What is human nature?

You know. Greedy.

Shannon considered this for a while.

If some people have more, she said, and most people have less, that proves just the opposite, that human nature isn't greedy.

Oh, he said, you're one of *them*, and refused to speak the rest of the way to the airport.

Yeah, I'm one of them.

Shannon drives past homes of the local ruling class. But the really important guys live in the U.S. The next most important ones live in Ontario and sometimes they come to visit and stay at the Bayshore, but they don't take cabs except in exceptional circumstances.

The local rulers are divided into the big bourgeoisie and the little bourgeoisie. The big guys made their money some generations ago by rum-running, war-profiteering, or some such activity. The little guys are just young entrepreneurs on their way up. The big bourgeoisie live mostly in Shaughnessy, though there are some on Drummond Drive and Belmont Drive, and the others live in the British Properties. They stay deliberately invisible so that the people won't know who the enemy is. Their children don't ride on buses and their houses are hidden by huge hedges and fences.

It isn't possible any longer to make it by the sweat of the brow. It probably never was. The ruling class inherited their property from ancestors who made it in illegal or semi-legal ways.

After them, there's the middle class, people like doctors, managers, directors, university presidents, some engineers, school superintendents. When ordinary people think of "making it," they mean making it to the middle class, the ruling class being too invisible to aspire to. The history of a newly industrializing country is as much that of an expanding middle class as of the rising bourgeoisie. Industry requires a great many technological skills, and also many people to teach them.

After the depression of the 1930s, there were only minor recessions until the 1960s. Thus there was a lot of new space being created in the middle class, and for those people born just before or during the war, it seems that aspiring to a higher class is just a normal way of life. They don't realize there was a time before, or that the time is now after, and stumble around drunk in the Ritz or Invermay, wondering what personal failing caused them to end up this way. There is no more room in the middle class for the sons of the working class (there never was any room for the daughters). Even the sons and daughters of the middle class are finding there is no further space for them, and so they are cast down into cannabis and hitch-hiking and they pretend for a time that it's groovy.

The shrinking of the middle class accounts as much as the war in Vietnam for the student rebellions of the late 60s. The students saw their future being taken away from them and they were furious, but they lost and are now docile and suckhole a lot since so few of them are going to make it. The rest will be busted into the working class or learn to like LSD and heroin.

The working class is the largest class but they don't know it and don't even think of themselves as a class very often. This class didn't lose anything economically during the 1960s except for some individual aspirations. Workers are protected from recessions by trade unions and labour laws and are in about the same shape as before. There have always been, however, some considerable number of workers who are not protected by either unions or laws. These are mostly women, but also farm labourers, fishermen, and taxi drivers. The women began an active struggle to improve their lot in the late 1960s and the movement is growing. However, as women's wages haven't changed much and prices have, it's possible that Women's Liberation is only doing a holding action; that is, keeping things at their previous level and not winning anything. Women do not get any support from the labour aristocracy, who are too busy protecting their privileges to heed the problems of the under-privileged and the unemployed.

The lowest class is the lumpenproletariat. There is always room at the bottom. They keep getting moved around but that doesn't affect the number, which grew in the late 1960s and appears to have stayed the same since then.

Only a few of them, however, are proper lumpens. The definition of lumpenproletariat, implied but never defined by Marx, is that they are people who will never be workers. They have found illegal or quasi-legal ways to make a living and are, therefore, not interested in being workers and have no need to be workers. Thus, there are a very few members of the lumpenproletariat in Canada. The largest group would be dope pushers who are not junkies, and pimps. There are also the bootleggers and the professional thieves.

These people are not poor. On the contrary, they have more money than even the middle-class, but they must live in the slums because it is easier to hide there and because that's where their customers are. A parasite must live on or near the body of its host.

These people are not interested in change. They have it really good and if it came to revolution, they would send their sons to fight for the continuation of the present system. A few of them will make it even higher. A pimp might get into the nightclub business and a good heroin dealer can even make it to the ruling class if he invests his money carefully and gets to know the right people.

This class – the pushers and pimps – are the proper lumpen-proletariat. Perhaps a more accurate term would be lumpen-*bourgeoisie* because, in fact, their interest lies with the ruling class rather than with the proletariat. There is, further, a peculiar synergistic relationship between them and the rulers. The rulers live in Shaughnessy and drink at the Vancouver Club and are really nice people, so they have to be able to hire someone to do their dirty work for them. Assassins and strike-breakers must be hired from somewhere. Further, at this time in the history of monopoly capitalism, it is very difficult for a young man to learn how to be a businessman since most small businesses have been strangled by corporations. Thus the sons of the rulers have nowhere to learn how to be rulers in capitalist society except by hanging around with the lumpenbourgeoisie for a short time. A young man from Shaughnessy might try his hand at selling hot cars or pushing dope while in high school so that he knows his way around the business world.

Besides the lumpenbourgeoisie, there are a great many other people at Columbia and Hastings, and they fall into at least four other groups.

Perhaps the largest group is women. All women at Columbia and Hastings are regarded as prostitutes. If they had any power they wouldn't be there, so they are made into prostitutes whether they want to be or not.

In spite of the way women are treated, the making of a hooker is not as easy a task as people would have you believe. There are three methods of persuasion which must be used all at once.

One is for a woman to get screwed by a succession of men in a cynical fashion, with or without her consent, which happens to all of us at one time or another. The lesson being taught is that fucking is meaningless and that no relationships with men are worthwhile and that love is a bunch of bullshit and that if you are indulging in a totally meaningless activity, you might as well get paid for it.

The second part of the breaking-down process is the offering of a great deal of money. The money only comes before a woman becomes a prostitute, and in most cases it is only the promise of money. When a woman actually becomes a hooker, she doesn't make all that much. Pimps take most of it, and pushers get all the rest because you have to take dope to stand it. Doctors also get a fair share due to venereal disease and the fact that all women get beat up but prostitutes can't go to the cops about it. Call girls make more money, but they have to live at a very high standard because that's what they are being paid to do, so they don't have much left over either and they, too, spend their surplus on pimps and pushers.

If these methods don't work, and they don't often work, women are simply beaten and raped into submission while still in their early teens.

Another large group of people on Columbia and Hastings who aren't lumpens are Indians. Some of them become proper lumpens, but not many because there is more overt racism in the slums than elsewhere. The Indians are there because they aren't allowed to go anywhere else. They are not allowed to live in good houses nor work in high-paying jobs. When a people are not allowed to work in an industrial society, they can go back to the previous mode of production, which is agriculture, or to hunting and gathering. This, however, requires land. The good lands have long since been taken away from the Indians by war, and all they were allowed to retain was the right to hunt and fish, which at one time could still provide subsistence. However, we are now witnessing the completion of the process by which Indians are not allowed to provide themselves with subsistence by these means, nor are they allowed to integrate into the majority economy. Inevitably, a minority of them end up at Columbia and Hastings, drinking away their poverty and despair.

Then there are the junkies and alcoholics who would straighten out if they felt they had some part to play in the society. There are also the merely unemployed looking for a cheap place to live.

Outside the pimps and the pushers (the lumpenbourgeoisie), these people are simply a reserve army of labour, kept out of the working class through no choice of their own. During times of labour shortage, they would quickly learn to work again, even the old people. As it is, nobody wants them, but they serve as an object lesson to employed workers about what happens to people who are surly to the boss, be that boss an employer or a husband.

Also at Columbia and Hastings, but invisible, are the blind, the crippled, the old, and the sick. These people live in the area because they can't afford to live anywhere else. They don't come out of their rooms very often. They also have skills, but nobody wants them.

First thing in the morning, a night driver borrowed Shannon's pen. After she had stood around waiting for her pen, he said he needed a cab home if she'd wait a bit longer. It was a good trip, east of four, so Shannon didn't mind. But then he started yelling at her about Women's Liberation, and was really uptight and abusive about it. He was quite drunk and drinking from a beer which Shannon also drank from, but that didn't explain his being so uptight about Women's Liberation.

Shannon chewed some gum before the next trip, which was in the same area. It was an old lady going to work at the Georgian Towers. Her son, she said, was a cab-driver. Then she complained about how she was old and how eight hours was too long for an old woman to work.

Does your son work the night shift? Shannon asked.

Yes.

He works 11 hours for five days then, and 12 hours on the sixth day.

Oh, but he's young.

He won't be for long after 67 hours a week, said Shannon.

It keeps him busy. If he wasn't working, he'd just be drinking, and this way he's not on the street and doesn't have time to drink.

Obviously the son didn't tell her anything about cab-driving.

If you weren't working, would you sit around drinking? Shannon asked.

No!

Then why assume your son will?

They all do.

Even the working class accepts the mythology about the working class.

Shannon got some coffee at the Travellers, then drove around looking for flags. Eventually she got a call to the Peter Pan. Two women, two men, and a child named Priscilla. The older woman had been beaten by her old man the night before, so she and Priscilla had left. The hippie-looking man had found them lost at Broadway and Alma, and took them downtown. Now they were going to catch the PGE for home. Priscilla was clutching some flowers someone had bought for her and trying to get rid of an ice cream cone.

The next fare was a flag on Burrard. The woman who waved was trying to pull a man out of a Volkswagen in which he was stuck headfirst. She finally got him out, and after arranging him in an upright position, she got into the cab. He stood around muttering drunkenly at her for a long time and she was very friendly but seemed relieved when he finally staggered off.

Look at me! she said to Shannon. I'm beautiful! Am I beautiful? I'm making a come-back.

Come-back to what? Shannon asked.

I don't know. I don't know. I don't know. Am I beautiful? Her laughter was tinged with hysteria. When she calmed down, she told Shannon she was a waitress. Her husband had left her two years before. She had hated him all along, but he was the best she could do and there was no way she could live without him when the children were smaller. Now he had left and she found that her fears had been justified: it was impossible to support two children on a woman's salary. She had been put in Crease Clinic for a while, but you can't do that and raise two children. The only solution was to get another husband. She was tired, weary down to the very depths, but make-up and false gaiety covered up the fatigue and men would never notice. Her hair was bleached to hide the grey, her face heavily made up to hide the fatigue, and her body girdled to hold up the sagging flesh. Altogether, she presented a picture of plastic gaiety. But there were no men around now and she could sag and laugh the bitter laugh men are never to hear. Am I beautiful?

I only want to grow old, she said. But there's all those years of schooling for the children, so I'm making a come-back. Am I beautiful? She laughed all the way home.

Shannon gave her a cigarette and guided her to her home, which turned out to be a dingy basement room with treacherous stairs leading down to it. Don't let them get you, Shannon said to her, leaving, and felt stupid for saying it. They had already got her.

Another passenger that day was a stewardess going to Denman Place. She was all perfect and plastic, but she did not laugh. Shannon asked her how she felt about the airlines using stewardess's bodies to sell tickets, and the woman thought it was okay. She also thought it was great that stewardesses were retired after 10 years. After all, old bodies were no good for selling tickets. She said if the airlines kept women on after 10 years, they would have to give them long service benefits, like free airplane tickets, which the men got.

Shouldn't women get these? Shannon asked. The woman replied that it cost money, and by the time they were 30, women just weren't attractive any longer, so by 35 they should be pastured out.

She was a very polite person, never lost her cool, and smiled prettily at Shannon throughout the conversation. Shannon talked more about women being moulded into plastic, made to behave like something they weren't, doing the phony act so men would find them pleasing. It was, after all, only men who had enough money to buy airplane tickets in any significant numbers. Women rode buses or stayed home.

The woman smiled her mannequin smile at Shannon and said: But we don't have to act or be phony – I assure you, this is the *real me*.

And Shannon realized with horror that it was.

In the summer, Evelyn said the house and the baby were driving her out of her mind, and she got another job as a receptionist. However, her boss turned out to be a sex maniac so she quit again almost immediately.

Both cars broke down, and in spite of the hours Bradley spent fixing them, they would not run consistently. They were old wrecks and should have been dumped years before, but fixing them made Bradley happy, so Evelyn was unfailing in her admiration and never complained about the constant breakdowns. Shannon, however, was not so loyal, and this made Bradley furious.

Having you in the house is like living with a wounded bear, he told her.

Shannon didn't feel like a wounded bear; she felt like a rag doll. Bradley said rag dolls didn't snarl and why didn't she try being human for a change. So when Shane asked her for coffee, she went, though she hated clever and cool young men, because he sometimes helped Bradley with car parts.

I love you, he said, holding out his hand across the table. He didn't mean it and Shannon knew he didn't. He wasn't capable of love. But Shannon saw that hands could transform into flesh the satin cloth she was made of, and the next morning it wasn't a stuffed doll sitting in the driver's seat.

Only, a woman cabbie made of flesh and blood is liable to be killed, whereas no one can get at a doll stuffed with old nylons. All day Shannon had the gnawing pain in her belly and was terrified she would get a call requiring her to walk into a pub. There they all were, the men who were treated like scum, the lowest of the low, but they always knew there was something they had power over, somebody they could make lower than themselves, and that was a woman. Seeing her walk into the pub, a slightly better grade of meat than they were accustomed to, they would all raise their heads slightly, like dogs, and the animal eyes would all shift in her direction.

At the Davie stand, a man fell down beside the car, but just as Shannon was getting out, he got up and fell into the back seat of the car, striking his head on the door frame as he did so. He said he wanted to go to the Broadway Hotel, but he looked dead so Shannon suggested she would take him to St. Paul's instead. He protested vehemently and would have got out, and Shannon thought that at the Broadway, at least, he wouldn't be falling onto concrete.

He was one of the hundreds of Columbia Street dwellers who fell on their heads. It was probably due to brain damage from drugs or wood alcohol. They didn't fall slowly down like normal people; they pitched forward head first like a diver leaping into a swimming pool. Only there was no swimming pool. The man had blood running down the side of his head and into his ear. Shannon wiped some of it off and then drove him to the Broadway. He paid and got out.

On the street, he paused to put on his sweater, but lifting his arm threw him off balance so that he dived head first under the car, his head hitting the pavement with a dull clunk. Shannon lifted him up and tried to make him sit on the sidewalk, but he got up immediately. She tried to hold him upright but he shook her off, and in so doing lost his balance again, falling with the same dull clunk. She didn't try to help him any more, just watched him get up and walk uncertainly into the Broadway, with blood running in thin red rivulets from about six different places on his head.

She got two coffees and went to see Gerald. When she came out, she was still 14th in the West End. She thought about going back to see Gerald and saying, Shane kissed me on the corner of Hastings and Nanaimo, and Gerald would reply, don't people usually kiss on the mouth? It wasn't funny enough to drown out the clunk of the man's head on the pavement. Anyway, she could no longer remember being kissed, only the man falling and falling and the blood running down his face.

A stuffed woman got in the car and there were tears running out of her button eyes.

Is anything wrong? Shannon asked.

It's my bird. Every day when I go out, my bird says kiss-kiss to me. This morning my bird didn't say kiss-kiss.

Oh well, Shannon said, birds have their bad days, too.

All the people walking around the West End looked like teddy bears with bright button noses and bright button eyes. Shannon thought how nice it would be to have no sound of flesh and bone on pavement, but to be like a rag doll hanging out in the rain, drenched through to the last bit of nylon stocking stuffing. Then she wished there was something she could say to Gerald that didn't sound like "I love you" but meant the same thing.

Evelyn, do you still love me?

Of course, Evelyn said. The baby had another cold and Evelyn, who had been up all night steaming the room, looked tired and confused, so Shannon went downstairs to sleep.

Shane only talked to her once more. He came into her basement room when she was in bed, and asked if she wanted to ball. She replied that she couldn't right then, but if he cared to hang around for a week, she might. Shane told her not to act like a 16-year-old and that she would either ball right then or not at all. So Shannon said regretfully he should stuff it in a knothole, and he went out, slamming the door.

August 1971

Shannon, in those early years, avoided the fancy hotels like the plague, feeling that the people in them were dangerous and vulgar. But the lady from zone seven was going to the Bayshore.

Are you married? she asked.

I don't answer that question, Shannon replied.

I don't blame you. Isn't this a dangerous job for a girl?

Naw, why? Were you thinking of applying?

The lady looked shocked. God no, she'd never be pushing hack, covered with sweat and wrinkled clothing on a hot afternoon. Shannon told her there weren't many problems, certainly fewer than in other women's jobs like, for example, nursing, where doctors and senile old men were allowed to pat nurses' bottoms and slaver over them, and the nurses were not allowed to mash guys in the chops and tell them to fuck off. The lady crouched warily in her corner as if she had inadvertently found herself in a cage with a lion.

At the Bayshore, a perfectly manicured and perfumed gentleman paid the fare and the lady rushed to him, even more determined to please than before, lest he cast her out and cause her to plummet to Shannon's level. The doorman closed the door so the gentleman wouldn't get his hands dirty.

After that, Shannon delivered some brown envelopes and also a young man who asked her if she wanted to ball. She declined politely, which incensed him and threatened his manhood, but it was a sunny summer afternoon and there wasn't anything he could do about it. Like all the others, he wasn't interested in sex, only in displaying his power, and Shannon should at least have got her feelings hurt.

It was too sunny for many people to be riding in cabs. Mostly Shannon sat on various stands daydreaming. Two of the new drivers came along to ask for advice on various matters, which

Shannon dispensed casually but eruditely. She had been telling passengers they had the privilege of riding with the rottenest driver in all of Vancouver, but now she thought maybe she wasn't so bad. She would get better and better until she would be the greatest cab-driver in all of Vancouver, if not all of Canada, and there would be legends told about her. Drivers sitting on downtown stands would sip coffee and tell new drivers the stories. Boy they sure don't make them like that any more . . .

Was it a big deal to be the greatest cab-driver in the world? Why wasn't it? A man going from the Blackstone to the bus depot told her she was the most beautiful cabbie he had ever seen.

Is that a big deal, Gerald?

She had persuaded him to come out of his room for a milk-shake at McDonald's. He said he had sworn never to go to McDonald's, but Shannon explained that having principles made him political instead of mystic, so they went to McDonald's. He looked rotten. He said he had been stoned for a week already and was very paranoid. She asked him why anybody would hate him, and he said she knew nothing about him, that in actuality he was very vain and thought himself important enough for many people to kill. Shannon told him people really were out to kill him, but for class, not individual, reasons. She was delighted to find he was vain, and told him about how she would be the greatest cab-driver in Vancouver, if not all of Canada. Gerald reckoned he would become famous sooner than she would. He also reckoned she would be upset he had spent her money on grass instead of boots. She told him he ought to have grass *and* boots, but he wouldn't take any more money. She assured him they were sure to become famous before they starved to death, and Gerald agreed they might, only it was very likely he would be famous first.

Two drunk people were sitting at the next table, and the woman was telling the man he was stupid and was wasting his whole life.

Shannon told Gerald she had gone to see M.A.S.H. and had run out in the middle of it. She was mostly upset by the fact that people would actually go to see such a cynical and sadistic movie, and had been intending to run the car off a bridge, but she had several days' earnings in her pocket which she wished to give to Gerald first. Before she found him, the need to disappear had gone away, and she hadn't continued looking for him that night. Gerald said it was too bad, he needed the money. The woman at the next table was still telling the drunk how stupid he was, and Shannon could see Gerald still thought he would be famous before she was.

Tourists don't get up until noon on Sundays, and it was only just after sunrise.

I'm taking up residence on the Blue stand, the radio said.

Roger. Expect to be there some time, do you?

I'll start a low-cost housing development.

11 and 38 moving to the West End, another voice said. He beat me at a game of crib on the Georgia so now we're moving to the West End for a rematch.

If we had one more on the B and G, we could play bridge.

Anyone for monopoly?

My bishop has just been stolen.

Does he want a cab?

Car 32 had been sitting on the Dev stand for an hour, he told Shannon. She got back in her car on Georgia and he moved off the Dev. Just then the despatcher called it, but since there was no one there now, Shannon got the second call on the Georgia. It was only a jerk and, 65 cents later, she was looking for a stand again. After considerable driving, she found room on the Davie. 32 was now on the St. Helen's and yelled at her that he had been sitting there since moving from the Dev, and now it was two hours since he had a trip. He fretted for a while and finally moved off, towards the West End. He hadn't even made it to the light when the despatcher called the St. Helen's. 32 swore into his mike, and Shannon picked up hers, expecting to answer for the second call. But then a voice yelled 48, 48 on the St. Helen's. 48 was speeding down the street, still half a block away from the stand. He's not on the stand yet, Shannon told the radio. I am, I am so, 48 yelled desperately, pulling onto the stand. But he was going too fast and couldn't turn properly with the mike in one hand, and there was an ugly sound as the car bounced off the fender of the truck parked just behind the stand. Davie, the despatcher said, and Shannon got the call, which was to the Yale. The man was going to the airport. Poor slob driving 48. Shannon didn't know him but he must be a new driver. An ex-driver now.

Sundays are always slow unless it snows, and it rarely snows in August in Vancouver. When she got back downtown, Karl Terry parked behind her on the Belmont stand and they sat talking for about half an hour. Karl said he didn't like driving because it was such a low-class job and people thought only jerks drove cabs. But there didn't seem to be any other jobs around. His wife had a managerial position with one of the department stores, but didn't make enough money for both of them to live on. Karl said he made more money than his wife did, but he worked longer hours.

They're right, we're jerks, Shannon said. Suckers. We get ripped off all the time.

Nobody rips me off, Karl said defensively.

I don't mean passengers, I mean owners, by not fixing cars . . .

But Karl wasn't listening. I rip them off, he said. Once a drunk lost a ten dollar bill on the seat. Do you think I gave it back to him? No, I kept it.

Come on, Karl. Everybody tells me that one. How come drunks go around dropping ten dollar bills in everybody's car but mine?

Another time, I'm on the Dev and there's this call girl. She told the man that she was from New West and that the fare was about $7, so he gives me $10. When he went away, she started laughing and gave me an address in the West End. When we get there, she says, give me the change. But I wouldn't give it to her. Goddamn whore. He gave me the money, not you, I told her.

You can't do anything about it, I told her. You were trying to cheat, I told her, and this will show you that cheating doesn't pay.

For chrissake, Karl. What were *you* doing but cheating?

She didn't get the money either, the goddamn whore.

What does that make you?

Irritably Karl got out and back into his car and went to find another stand. Shannon never did get a call from the Belmont.

It started raining about noon, which helped business some. Shannon was sent to an address in the West End. She didn't feel like getting wet and, gripped with inertia, would not get out of the car to open the door for the woman, who looked physically able to open the door by herself. But the woman just stood there, and after some time, Shannon dragged herself out in the rain and opened the door.

I've never opened a car door in my life, the woman said, and I'm not going to start now. Hotel Vancouver, please. I have to go to work today though it's Sunday. We're having a meeting. Normally, I only work six days a week, but today we're having a meeting which I must attend. Important people have to work harder, you know.

Employees' entrance?

Oh, no! The front door. I don't have to use the servants' entrance. I'm a manager. I'm sorry, I didn't notice before that you were a girl. But I've never opened a car door in my life. Some of the drivers take such a long time to open the door, which is a pity. I always say it helps to be courteous. Politeness is what gets you ahead in this world. Look at me. I'm a manager and there aren't many women managers, I can tell you.

In August, the Japanese government refused to devalue the yen. Shannon didn't understand the reasons why the Americans wanted the yen devalued, but she did understand that there were problems within the American empire. Japan, instead of acting like a proper colony, was now looking like a rival capitalist power. From one point of view, this was a nice development as dissension among capitalists might lead to their downfall. Europe also, by forming the Common Market, was making an effort to set up a capitalist empire in rivalry with the U.S. On the other hand, there had already been two great wars between rival capitalist enterprises.

The American reaction to this threat from within its own ranks was to line up more allies, and the admission of China into the U.N. was not an indication of improvement, but of unhealthy collusion between empires. Similarly, the sudden friendship between Canada and the Soviet Union was only a sign that the Americans wanted more allies to use against incipient rebellion in their own ranks. The U.S.S.R. was having similar problems keeping their own rebellious colonies in hand. Also, surly Russian workers, bitter because of continuing food shortages, could not provide the precision manufactured goods which could be obtained from the U.S.

Thus in October of 1971, Kosygin, premier of all the Russias, came even unto Vancouver. To the Canadian people, who had never quite understood the necessity of hating the Russians, the visit was quite welcome. All the people Shannon asked about it, down to the drunkest drunks, knew about the visit, which was amazing all by itself. They also expressed relief and pleasure, though no one was interested in Kosygin and didn't care if be lived or died. It was simply an expression of relief that the cold war was finally over. No more air raid shelters, no more school children crouching under desks, waiting for destruction to rain down from the sky. Canadians had talked about the American dream, but they had experienced it mostly as fear of war and annihilation.

Shannon was pleased about the visit for the same reasons as everyone else. However, as the two days of the visit wore on, she became quite irritable. Kosygin rode around in a cavalcade of about a dozen black cars with motorcycle escort, and all traffic was stopped whenever he passed by. It seemed to Shannon that he made an extraordinary number of trips because wherever she was going, she had to stop and wait for the black cars to pass by. The end of the cold war just looked to her like a traffic jam and nothing more.

On the morning of his departure, she stopped to watch the Jewish demonstration at the Hotel Vancouver at 8:30 a.m. Kosygin was well hidden in the bowels of one of those black cars and was probably not aware of the demonstration.

The war went on as before.

Shannon, driving down Blenheim one day in October, looked up and found that all the leaves were gone from the trees. Immersed in fatigue, she had not seen them change colour and had not noticed the weather getting colder and the rain more insistent. There are not so many autumns in one's life that you can afford to miss one just like that. She had a cold for weeks, and finally one Saturday morning found she couldn't get out of bed, so she lay there listening to the phone ringing. It wouldn't stop, so she answered it and told the office she had the flu and put down the phone while the person on the other end was still yelling and cursing. She got Evelyn to phone them in the afternoon to say she wouldn't be in for several days. She was sick for a week, at the end of which time she owed an owner $40 for being ill. She didn't, of course, have $40, so they told her she couldn't work there any more. She went back to bed for two more days, and in the end they agreed she could come to work if she turned in $5 at the end of each shift until she paid $40.

Bradley was out of town again. He had gone miserably, but there was another construction job available at Lornex Mines, and they were penniless once again so he had to go. He got drunk out of his mind the night before leaving and was still drunk when Evelyn put him on the plane in the morning.

Daddy barfed in the parking lot, the baby said proudly.

Evelyn came downstairs several times to offer Shannon nursing care, but Shannon refused in churlish tones and slept for days and days. In her sleep, she could hear the baby saying "Why" over and over again, and Evelyn yelling "no" and "don't" at her at regular intervals. Although Shannon didn't think it was a good idea, the baby came downstairs and played in her bed during her times of semi-wakefulness. She made a lot of noise and brought all her toys with her, so at any one time Shannon might find three dolls, two tractors, a broken car, a bulldozer complete with grading equipment, a hammer, three empty boxes, 456 building blocks, three books, and a slightly used paint-by-number set in her bed. The baby talked continuously now, always very loudly. At first she would come down looking for Bradley, who had always been the most important person in her life.

Badley? she would ask Shannon and Shannon would tell her to go speak to her mother.

Badley's away at work, she told Shannon. Mommy misses him. *Hard* work.

Do you miss him?

Nope, shaking her head furiously, but every few minutes she would ask again when Badley would be home.

She also sang a lot, mostly nonsense words to her own rhythm, but also Itsy Bitsy Spider and This Old Man. She liked playing in the sink best, and now that Shannon was too weak to banish her, she could spend hours splashing water, breaking cups and talking to herself about it. Get some tomato juice, clunk, pour it in the sink, clunk, get some orange juice, pour it in the sink. Shatter.

Does she bother you? Evelyn asked apologetically.

No. She talks more intelligently than most of my passengers. She misses Bradley something awful. Would you reach me that bottle of brandy? Does he mind being called Badley?

Yes, he tries to convince her to call him Daddy, which she does most of the time. He likes being a daddy. Strange man, I don't know how I came to marry him. Do you drink much?

You were always such a prude. I drink as much as I need to. No, not quite as much as I need to.

It's all ridiculous, Evelyn said. We can't just hardly talk to each other and live in the same house.

I can't afford to move.

I don't want you to move; I want to talk.

I don't have anything to say.

Why don't you quit that stupid job?

What would I live on then?

You could get another job.

All jobs are stupid.

Some are worse.

Evelyn, I'm tired.

Get some sleep then and come up for supper later.

I don't want supper.

Come and talk then. I miss Bradley too.

I don't want to talk.

What do you want?

I want to be left alone.

Bewildered when Evelyn left, she thought – but there was a time I loved her, there was a time I couldn't wait to talk to Evelyn, to have supper with Evelyn, to be with Evelyn, and no thought was quite so exciting until shared with Evelyn.

The next day she asked Evelyn if she could still come to supper and Evelyn said of course, if she didn't mind lamb chops and broccoli. Evelyn didn't want any brandy so Shannon sipped it by herself while Evelyn cooked supper and tried to keep the baby out of the sink.

Do you know how long we've been friends? Shannon asked.

Eleventy seven years. Then why don't we talk?

Because you nag Bradley.

I don't, Evelyn said. Any more than he needs nagging, that is. Tell me about your job. Tell me what you think about when the alarm rings at 3:30 a.m.

Shannon sipped at her brandy, considering that if she told Evelyn how it all was, maybe Evelyn would tell her what was happening and how to stop it.

The baby threw a glass on the floor and smashed it. Evelyn grabbed her and put her in her room, then started sweeping up the broken glass. After which she discovered the broccoli had burned. Shannon got the sobbing baby from her room and tried to convince her everything was going to be all right.

Over supper, Evelyn kept apologizing about the burned broccoli. Shannon said she needn't have put the baby in her room, since she had been playing and hadn't intended to break the glass. Evelyn said she had to get her out of the way so she wouldn't cut herself, and Shannon replied the baby didn't know that, but thought she was being punished. Evelyn said Shannon sure knew a lot about child-raising for one who didn't help much, and Shannon took her brandy bottle and went back to her room.

The waitresses at the Peter Pan were the most beaten bunch of women Shannon had ever seen. The one giving Shannon a bag full of food said she didn't see why the man hadn't called a restaurant closer by, but he had yelled at her on the phone and so she had done his bidding.

I don't know what to do. He probably won't pay you.

Shannon shrugged and paid for the food. It was to go to room 103 of the Broadway Hotel. Since it was early morning, the outside door was locked, but the Chinese clerk opened it for her and told her 103 was upstairs.

A tiny woman with dead eyes opened the door for Shannon. She had hastily thrown on some clothes, but the man was still naked. He had a swollen pig's face and was enormously fat so that his breast hung down to his belly and his belly over his thighs.

Hey, you're kinda cute, he bellowed at Shannon. Come into bed with me.

Shannon walked out into the hallway for a minute, leaning against the wall to take deep breaths, but then she had to go back in for the money. The man handed her a $100 bill. She had never seen one before. The beaten woman stared at the bill too, and then she and Shannon looked at each other. It was only ugly pigs who had $100 bills. The only way the beaten woman could acquire even part of it was by tolerating the repulsiveness of the pig, vomiting afterwards, and shutting it all out with heroin.

Shannon, of course, hadn't enough change, so the pig bellowed into the phone at the desk clerk who was called a cocksucking Chinaman because he didn't run fast enough.

Downstairs in the lobby, there was a coffee machine. When she got paid, Shannon threw a dime into the machine. The clerk told her that all his customers weren't like that cocksucking Jew.

She didn't say anything to anyone about it all. But when she was cashing in, 72 told her about how he had thrown out a "squaw" for exposing herself, and only then did Shannon get angry and start yelling. He had to call her a woman, she told the guy, and if she was exposing herself it was because she was usually paid to do it. Didn't they all do what they were paid to do? That week a drunk at the Ritz was paying taxi drivers $6 an hour to listen to him talk. Hadn't they all been rushing down to the Ritz? Calling him Sir and pretending to be interested in his drunken blather for $6 an hour. Racist fucking whores.

Seventy-two said he hadn't gone to the Ritz. The other drivers looked at her in wonder but didn't say anything. It was so rare to hear any kind of conversation in the drivers' room, let alone any passion.

The next day she found Gerald.

I'm sorry I was sick, she said. For the last few nights I looked for you in all those all-night places, after they told me you'd been chucked out for not paying your rent. All those all-night places. In each place, there were all these men, the lowest of the low, and if I'd stayed any longer, they'd have trampled me.

I know, said Gerald, that's what keeps them moving. Their hatred for women. And Chinese.

Chinese? Why?

I don't know.

Where do all the women go?

Which women?

Poor women. There are more poor women than there are men. Where do they all go?

I don't know. It's a class thing, you know, like you said. Fighting. I was just crossing the street and I hadn't had any meat for a couple of months and this car blew the horn at me, I guess I was kind of walking slow, I was hungry. I got furious, insanely furious, and threw a rock at him. I'd have killed him if I could. I'd never done that before.

While he was sleeping in Stanley Park, his welfare money for the month had been stolen and he'd gone for two weeks without a penny. People who don't have a place to sleep at night walk around a lot. Few hotels will let them sit in the lobby in the evening, and none will after midnight. The bus depot and the CNR station are locked until 6 a.m. That leaves the CPR station, but too many ragged people can't crowd the place every night or they'd all get thrown out. Most of them walk. Walk and walk and walk. There is nowhere to sit down, nowhere to get warm. There are no public washrooms. For the price of a coffee, they can get out of the rain for a while, but many cafes won't let them linger over their coffee, and a person who falls asleep is instantly thrown out.

It's just as well you couldn't find me, Shannon said. I think you were getting the idea you could trust me so you might as well find out now as later that I'm untrustworthy.

I had no money for almost two weeks. But it's easy. You don't have to deliver, you only have to look as if you will and they'll buy you food and coffee. I ate that way for a week.

Huh?

I guess I look desperate and so these guys come up and say I'm kinda cute, and they buy me some food. But I don't have to go home with them.

Wouldn't anyone feed you for nothing?

Are you crazy? Once a guy did and I thought it was for nothing but he turned out to be a religious nut. I ran away.

Better to give up your body than your soul. Do the homosexuals only pick on desperate looking guys?

I don't know. I suppose.

Well, so now you know how it feels. Only, women have to deliver.

I know.

What are you reading?

Ken Kesey.

Christ. Did they buy you some yogurt?

No. Hamburgers.

Christ. That's why. If you ate better, you'd read Marx and get a job. You look terrible.

November morning. Another plane had been hijacked.

There hadn't been a murder in Vancouver in the night, thus stopping the week's record number of murders. The night before, in the Zanzibar, a man wearing a blond wig and fake moustache shot another man while the drums rolled for the final number. The man who killed two teenagers who were hitch-hiking home from a rock concert at the PNE said he had drunk a case of beer and didn't remember what happened.

There had been a fire on the 20th floor of 1850 Comox.

At Pigeon Park, a group of people with several guitars played and sang all night while drinking coke and vanilla.

In the doorway of 43 E. Hastings, two drunk kids were mopping blood off the head of a man lying there. The despatcher told Shannon he couldn't call an ambulance because if the injured person didn't pay for it, whoever called must pay the ambulance cost. Shannon asked him to call the cops. The man bleeding on the sidewalk told the drunk kids that three men had jumped him for no reason at all.

Shannon drove a nurse to work at St. Paul's. The nurse told Shannon it was a nice morning. Two women, drinking coffee, went to work at Simpson Sears. They told Shannon and each other it was a nice morning.

Then another drunk. He told Shannon it was a nice morning and asked if she was married. Then he said she was the funniest looking person he had ever seen and he laughed and laughed. She asked him why and he said because she had hair sticking up and wore glasses and she was a *woman*. Shannon told him half the population were women, but he continued being amazed and amused.

Another drunk going home asked Shannon where he could get a woman.

What kind? Shannon asked.

Any kind. Just a fuck. What about you?

You don't care what the woman looks like, right?

Yeah.

Nor what she thinks, nor if she is happy, nor whether she is rich or poor or anything like that. Just so she has a hole.

Yeah, yeah.

Well, why not stick it in a knothole?

What?

Go inside and play with yourself.

You think so?

It's the only solution.

By that time, offices were opening, so people gave her brown envelopes to deliver and told her it was a nice day. About noon, she was in front of an apartment by UBC, tired and with a pain in her abdomen. Finally a well-dressed young man came out of the apartment carrying a box. The address he gave Shannon turned out to be a pet hospital, into which he disappeared with the box, after telling Shannon to wait. In a short time he was back, minus the box.

Sick dog? she asked.

Yeah. Suddenly he burst into tears. Shannon awkwardly put her arm around his shoulder while he sobbed and said I'm sorry, I'm sorry, between sobs.

It's okay, Shannon said, patting him. We in Women's Liberation figure it's okay for men to cry. You go ahead and cry. She searched her pockets for a clean Kleenex to give him.

Thank you, thank you, he sobbed.

Shannon sat, holding him, watching the meter tick. If he cried much longer it would be a very good trip.

My wife is away, he sobbed. How will I tell her?

Finally he straightened out and stopped crying, except for the occasional sniffle, and asked her to take him back to the apartment.

The next passenger was a woman going downtown.

Christ, my hands are a mess, she said.

Did you fall?

Christ, no. I was in a fight.

Did you win?

Did I win! You don't see me with a black eye!

The other woman has a black eye?

Goddamn right she has.

Where did this happen?

That goddamn dp place.

Which one?

On Granville. You know the one.

No. Peter Pan?

That's not a goddamn dp place. Farther down. By the St. Helen's.

Mr. Food's?

That's the one. This hustler called me a filthy whore, for no reason. I beat her. Dragged her outside. Kicked her in the face. Filthy whore. I'd have killed her if the cops hadn't come.

What did the cops charge you with?

Nothing. Why should they? It's not illegal to fight if you win.

The poor and downtrodden should not fight each other, Shannon said.

I'm not poor! I sure showed that goddamn whore. Say, I'm sorry for swearing like this. Do you mind?

Christ, no, Shannon said. I swear all the time myself and use "fuck" frequently.

You can't say that! It's an awful word. You shouldn't use that word. It's a terrible word.

Not as terrible as kicking people in the face, I reckon.

Another cold and black November morning. How come I'm always tired, Shannon moaned to the blackness, but without conviction, since she had long ago accepted her constant fatigue as normal.

The Sportsman had burned in the night. A stove in the kitchen blew up and the kitchen was completely destroyed. No one was hurt, but staff were laid off for several months and it was almost Christmas.

A paddy wagon was loading up with people from Pigeon Park.

Four people asked Shannon if she was married, if she thought it wasn't a nice day, and how was the cab business. A regular, ordinary Sunday morning.

About 8 a.m. she was sent to a shop on Fraser because only a lady driver was acceptable. A drunk and dirty woman, with urine on her white slacks, came out of a shop and asked Shannon to carry her piggy bank because it was too heavy for her. It was a large and heavy piggy, and the woman then asked Shannon to open it, but Shannon couldn't. The woman had cut a hole in it with a nail file, and got out several dollars worth of silver that way, but she couldn't get at the rest. She asked Shannon to take her to a bootlegger, but Shannon told her she didn't know of any. The conversation was repeated about 15 times. Finally, after Shannon told her to get out of the car, the woman gave her an address, whimpering that her husband beat her and she didn't want to go home, but to a bootlegger. Shannon offered to drive her to a hospital, but she just whimpered about a bootlegger and Shannon drove her home.

At the house, Shannon asked if the woman wanted her husband to know about the piggy bank. The woman whimpered that it didn't matter, he would beat her anyway. By this time the man had seen them. He was huge and angry and he seized his wife by the arm, jerked her around, and yelled that he would kill her. Shannon, holding the ungainly piggy, told the man to let her go, which he did, and then the woman rushed away somewhere into the depths of the house.

Your wife is a sick woman, Shannon said to the man. He was huge and angry and didn't look as if he had ever been a human being. He said his wife was a drunk and how much money had Shannon got from her this time? Shannon said, she's a sick woman and it won't help to beat her because she doesn't have any brains left. She also told him he had driven his wife crazy and now he had to look after her, no matter how much it cost him. The man didn't say anything more, but sat down at the kitchen table, holding his head in his hands. Shannon leaned over him and said: She had better not get hurt, this sick woman. If she is hurt, everyone will know you did it, and I will testify in court that I heard you threaten her. You're as ugly as this piggy here, and you drove her crazy and burned out her brains, and if anything happens to her, you will be hung, do you hear me? The man shuddered, still holding his head in his hands, and when Shannon left the house, she heard the sounds of his sobbing.

After that, more drunks. Shannon asked them not to call her chick, broad, pet, honey, sweetheart, baby, love. One of the drunks then decided she was a bisexual and said it was bisexuals who really turned him on. Shannon pulled him out of the car, but he ran around to her side of the car and leaned against the door, telling her what a good fuck he was.

You make me sick, Shannon said. He said that bisexuals really turned him on. The thought of touching you, even, makes me want to puke, Shannon said. But he said that wasn't possible, he was such a good fuck, leaning on the car door and trying to unzip his pants. Shannon put the car in gear and moved forward slowly. He ran alongside, still holding the door, so Shannon drove a bit faster and finally he fell away from the door. She stopped to see if he was hurt. He got up and seized the door again and said bisexuals really turned him on. This time she shook him off by rocking the car back and forth, and drove away without checking to see if he had been injured.

The despatcher was calling for a car in six, but Shannon couldn't stand it for another minute and went to the Black Cat instead. It was crowded and the only space was at the counter. Shannon was shaking badly and couldn't put cream and sugar in her coffee, so the woman sitting beside her did it for her. She explained to the woman that she was a cab-driver and had just had some bad customers.

The woman brushed away her thanks and said she had been pleased to help. She said most people thought cab-drivers were stupid, but she had this really stupid daughter so she knew what *really* stupid was, and her daughter was too stupid to even drive a car. It was because the daughter hadn't been fed enough protein when she was a baby that she turned out stupid. She was now 29 years old and unbelievably stupid.

What does she do that is stupid? Shannon asked.

She doesn't do anything, that's how stupid she is. Bad, too. She doesn't have any friends. She sometimes makes a friend, but I tell them what an evil bitch she is and they soon find out. It's my fault, really. I didn't feed her enough protein when she was a baby.

Does she work?

She had a job, but now she can't find another one. She was a manager in a dress shop, but I made her quit.

How can she be a manager if she is stupid?

I'll tell you a secret. *All* managers are stupid. It wasn't the right kind of job for her, I told her, and made her quit. She didn't want to quit and said she liked her job, but I worked on her and worked on her and finally made her quit.

Why did you make her quit?

It wasn't the right kind of job for her. She should be where she could meet some men, though what man would want an evil bitch like that, I don't know. In the dress shop she met only women. There's no young people there and she should be where she can meet men. She doesn't have any friends either, she's that dumb. She's really dumb. I bought her a house, you know. I've done everything for her.

Why?

Would you leave a crippled dog lying on the street? Then, do you know what? I buy her a house, in Richmond it was, and she won't let me in it. I had to get a lawyer.

Why did you want to get in it?

Why, to see that she was taking proper care of it, of course. She wanted to put the furniture in places other than where it should be, and you should have seen what she did to the kitchen!

Maybe she liked it that way.

What does she know what she likes? Maimed and evil. I have to follow her around and look after her because she's too stupid to live. And do you think she's grateful? She wouldn't even let me in the house, after I bought it for her. Do you know why?

No, Shannon said helplessly. Why?

She is ashamed of me because I'm lame.

Shannon fell in love with Ronnie in October but, preoccupied as are all drivers with making money, he didn't notice until several weeks had gone by. He worked the night shift and started work just as Shannon was going home, and Shannon started work just as he was going home, so there wasn't much they could do about it. For a few days she met him at the Black Angus early in the morning and was late for work and had to suffer the displeasure of the office. There were always a lot of drivers in the Black Angus and they all leered at Shannon, so that she felt stupid about holding Ronnie's hand under the table. Conversations with most men convinced her that both sex and women were remarkably filthy and that a decent young man would not have anything to do with either one except under the pressure of dire biological need.

Next after women, the drivers hated people of races other than their own. Sometimes Shannon would give them impassioned speeches and tell them what suckers they were for blaming their troubles on women and Indians, thus allowing themselves to be more freely ripped off. She talked to them about the necessity for organizing. But it was 4 a.m. and the men had been driving all night and they worked 70 hours a week and the only way they could stay awake was to hype themselves up in some fashion, for which purpose only hatred works sufficiently well. If they were to talk about love or organizing they would fall asleep and never make it to work again. Hatred helped them survive and, at the same time, prevented them from improving conditions in order to escape the necessity for hatred. They didn't, furthermore, think of it as hatred, but as the normal way ordinary people thought in this society.

Ronnie assured her he wasn't a racist and, in truth, in their private conversations he didn't appear to be a racist. Probably only totally degenerate people, of whom there are many, are racists as individuals. As individuals, most people can't really argue about the fact that all human beings are more or less the same in certain basic aspects, and that all human beings are different in other aspects. It requires the peculiar interaction of the group to set up an atmosphere where racism is not only allowable but mandatory, so that any individual feels like a total fink for not seeing and accepting what is so obvious to everyone else.

Shannon told Ronnie unhappily that she didn't like those early morning conversations in the Black Angus, and he was relieved since he was embarrassed by her berating the other drivers for racism and sexism and lack of solidarity. It was allowable so long as they didn't yet know she was his girlfriend; however, since they didn't know, they each tried to hustle her.

Finally Shannon took a day off in the middle of the week so she could sleep with Ronnie, but she resented losing money because of him, so he took an hour off each evening to come and visit her at home. This affected his sheets and made him unhappy. Shannon pointed out that workers who worked only eight hours got a lunch break and a coffee break. Ronnie said he knew that, but cab-drivers couldn't do that and still turn in high sheets, and the sheet always provided an irrefutable argument.

He already did take a break most evenings when he went to the Royal for a beer with some other drivers, and this he refused to give up. Shannon didn't see that he should give up his male friends for her. But there were those sheets.

Besides that, Shannon was having birth control problems. She asked the doctor for an IUD but, because of her bleeding problems, he said an IUD was out of the question. For her previous sporadic encounters she had used a diaphragm or simply trusted to luck, but this definitely would not work for regular sex. The only method left was the pill, but on the pill her breasts hurt and she felt irritable and water-logged. She complained bitterly to Ronnie about it, but he said that was her problem. He told her the office had phoned to yell at him about his low sheets, and he began stopping by less often. She told him that if money was more important than she was, she would be quite pleased to quit taking the fucking pill, and soon the visits ceased altogether.

The affair had only lasted a few weeks. One morning, about a month later, someone yelled her name at the Black Angus. Shannon was barely awake and it took her a few minutes to recognize Ronnie. She had learned every detail of his body and now he was a stranger.

She didn't tell Bradley or Evelyn about it, but she did tell Gerald because Gerald asked her if he should get a job driving cab.

Given up the romance of the street? Shannon asked.

Survival, not romance. I actually walked by Canada Manpower the other day.

Don't get a job as a cab-driver. It fucks up all your relationships. If Ronnie and I weren't cab-drivers, we'd have lived happily ever after.

I loved him, she said, and felt bewildered remembering she had loved him. I watched him walk across the room and the slow sad music I thought I would never hear, began again. Each morning I went to work drunk on the morning sun and the songs of the birds and smiled dreamily at all the passengers. Now I worry again about the sheet and I feel myself growing coarser and greyer every day and I've been waking up drunk every morning, only on booze now, because mornings and music are no longer enough.

Shannon's first passengers were three tall and good-looking men from the Bayshore, and she was irritated by them because men from the Bayshore were always taller and healthier and had better teeth than those from the Cecil or the Blackstone. They were going to the airport, which was a good trip, so she didn't tell them they irritated her and even agreed cheerfully it was a nice morning, though it wasn't. She wouldn't tell, however, whether or not she was married.

Then she got a man who said he was a football player from L.A. (after he told her it was a nice morning and wasn't it a dangerous job for a girl). He said he had played for the Lions in 64 when they won the Grey Cup. He said the Lions were a joke, and that Vancouver didn't want to put up the money for first draft choices.

Did you hear about the riot at the PNE last night? he asked.

Oh yeah. The rock and roll revival.

Them crazy hippies wrecked the stadium.

Shannon said they could hardly be hippies, since it was a rock and roll revival, and he replied that anyone who wrecked a stadium must be a hippie.

Don't insult hippies, Shannon said. I am one myself.

But she said it without conviction. Hippies didn't pay back student loans. Or maybe hippies only came in groups. You couldn't have just one hippie. Or maybe it was that women couldn't be hippies all by themselves. Any woman accompanied by a hippie man was automatically a hippie, but by herself a woman wasn't anything.

The next morning, the first fare was a drunk who left behind a pound of No. 1 Canada West spring wheat. This provided a conversation piece; instead of asking Shannon why she was a woman or commenting on the weather, people asked why she was carrying around a pound of No. 1 Canada West spring wheat. This made her remarkably cheerful. She asked them their opinion of the war, but not one of her passengers knew there was a war on. When Shannon said it was between India and Pakistan, people just said: what, again?

Two loggers from the Blackstone went to buy a bottle on Gore Avenue early in the morning before the liquor store opened. They told Shannon that Jason had been in the business for 20 years and had two kids at UBC.

They also told Shannon about the only woman they had ever known who drove a logging truck. She was Bailey's daughter, who used to get drunk on weekends and clean up on all the men in the bar. She had two children, they told Shannon, a boy and a girl, only the girl was a boy, too. This didn't seem to bother Bailey's daughter, the men told Shannon, but then both the boy and the girl-boy got into heroin, so Bailey's daughter took an overdose.

Shannon spent most of the day looking for washrooms and didn't turn in much of a sheet. Ronnie had been gone for two weeks and the gut ache was back.

December 1971

Added to the black and cold morning was snow. Not much, but enough to make the despatcher repeat all morning about driving with care and concentration.

At the Skillett, a drunk woman got in the cab. Surrey, she told the man with her, and it will be about $4. Is that so? he asked Shannon. Shannon said it depended on where in Surrey, and that it could be as much as $8. He gave her $5 and went back to the Skillett. The woman then gave Shannon an address in five and demanded back $3. Shannon was relieved because she didn't want to drive to Surrey in the dark and snow. Someone in Richmond was calling for a tow truck because he couldn't get out of a snow-filled ditch.

There wasn't anything happening in five, so Shannon drove back downtown. At Main and Prior, a woman was lying in the snow beside a telephone pole at such a weird angle Shannon thought she was dead. But when she walked over to her, she saw that the woman was smoking a cigarette. Her purse, with all its contents scattered over the snow, was lying beside her, and she was covered with dirt and dried blood.

Pick up my purse, the woman ordered, puffing on her cigarette. Shannon picked up all the stuff and put it in the purse, checking the bankbook as the woman ordered to see if it had a $2 bill in it. Then she helped the woman to the car.

St. Paul's or VGH?

18th and Knight.

You gotta go to a hospital.

No! The woman panicked and then calmed herself with an effort. Smiling craftily, she said: If my daughter thinks I need to go to a hospital, she will take me.

Does your daughter live at 18th and Knight?

Yes. Still the crafty smile.

What the hell. Shannon drove her to a broken-down apartment building.

It's two floors up, the woman said. Can you help me?

Why don't I just go and get your daughter? She might decide you should go to the hospital right away.

But the woman was already scrambling out of the car, almost falling in her hurry. Shannon had no choice but to hold her up while they climbed up two sets of creaking stairs.

The lock on the door had been broken off fairly recently, but the woman quickly went inside, shielding the door with her body so Shannon wouldn't notice. Then she stood in the middle of a desperately dingy room, looking at Shannon with a terrible plea. There was no daughter.

You live alone in this mean and dingy room, Shannon said accusingly. Come on, I'll take you to a hospital.

No! What can they do? She smiled pleadingly. Tell me your car number and if I don't feel good, I'll call you. Please.

Promise you'll call?

Promise. I'll call you if I don't feel good.

Oh Christ. Shannon gave her a card and stumbled down the stairs. There wasn't anything to be done.

The next woman was sober and going to work at the YWCA. She told Shannon she had hurt her leg and should be off for two weeks, but the Y was a Christian organization and had only allowed her two days off. All the same capitalists, she said, Christians or not. But she tried to do her job well and was proud if allowed to do so, as are most workers.

The next one was also a worker going to Burnaby. He also took pride in doing his job well. These are the people, and there are millions of them, who will take power after the revolution.

It had been the man's first daughter's birthday, so the second daughter had a party for her. But when everybody was ready to go home, this guy wasn't, so his son-in-law had dropped him off at a nightclub. There he had danced with every woman who would dance with him, and had a great deal more to drink. In the morning he went to the Skillett to eat and, after many coffees, judged himself sober enough to get home. He told Shannon about his job at the mines, his bosses, other workers, and they laughed most of the way down Hastings. At the house he only had enough money for the fare and apologized for not being able to tip.

That's all right, Shannon told him. Driving you was a pleasure.

Can I kiss you?

On the cheek.

He kissed her and the warmth stayed with her the rest of the day, and she didn't mind driving drunks or even musicians going to the Queen E, and she didn't mind everyone saying it was a nice day and asking if she was married.

She told people there was a war on and few of them had been aware of it. It was between India and Pakistan, and that didn't really make it a war since no white people were being killed. When she told people it was a war nevertheless, they said there were always wars there. Three people gave her virtuous speeches about how all wars were bad. Would it be better if people kept getting killed by the Pakistani army and the refugees got to number even more than seven million? Nobody ever wins, these people said. But somebody always wins.

Almost Christmas. The season of joy. The traffic got worse and worse and people gradually more maniacal, so that by Christmas Eve, drivers could just barely restrain themselves from squashing to death everyone who crossed their path. There were more drunks, both driving and walking, and a great many more people crossing over the edge of despair. Murder, suicide, mental breakdowns, divorce, heart attacks, child beatings, ulcers, and all the other symptoms of a disintegrating society were much more prevalent during this time.

Early in the morning the traffic was still tolerable, but women cab-drivers were well advised not to antagonize customers, even when those customers were drivers themselves.

Jeremy was a UBC student who drove cab during the Christmas break. Shannon drove him home one morning at 5 a.m. It was dark and cold and Jeremy told her he understood women, so she felt for the cold comfort of the tire iron under the seat.

Do you like driving cab? he asked.

It's a job, Shannon replied.

You can't say "it's a job" like that. That's how men say it.

It's still a job.

All the female drivers really like it.

They may be well advised to say so.

He was in business administration but he understood women and he didn't, he told Shannon, drive cab for the sake of driving cab, since no self-respecting person would try to live on the wages. No, he understood women. That was how he made a living. Working his way through college.

Shannon told him he was a parasite, which upset him a great deal, and it was dark and cold at 5 a.m. and totally deserted at UBC and the tire iron wouldn't be all that much help. So she smiled at him in the dark and told him he was clever and that guys like him were the ones who made it, while ordinary cabbies were just stunned.

It was daylight when she went into the Peter Pan to yell taxi. The man who followed her out asked her if she was a boy or a girl, which she didn't feel obliged to answer. He told her to take him to Broadway and Oak, and then he asked what she thought of the weather, which she also didn't answer. At Broadway and Oak it was easier to let him off on the wrong side of the street, so she asked him if she should turn around or would he mind walking across the street. Most people would have minded, but he said: I'll walk, I'm no cripple.

So then she smiled at him and one ought never smile at passengers.

Hey, he said, you're a nice girl! Want to sleep with me?

No. If you knew I was a girl, why did you ask me if I was a boy or a girl?

For fun. I knew you were a girl because I wouldn't drive with no long-haired boy.

I'm sorry I took you here then.

I had this long-haired boy once, and to boot, he was Chinese. I wouldn't ride with him. You wouldn't ride with dirt would you?

Unfortunately, I just have. Get out of my cab.

He got out, laughing. He had won, since he was already at his destination.

Several more men asked if she wanted to ball, and they also commented on the weather in the same bored tone of voice. The traffic got worse and worse as the day wore on. It was worst in the

Abbott zone around Woodward's, and since it was nearly impossible to get to anywhere, there were masses of people waiting for cabs and most of them never got one.

No pick ups in the Abbott zone, the despatcher said, like every afternoon. Like every afternoon, everyone picked up. Except Shannon who never booked into zones until she was there, never cleared until the passengers were out of the car, and never picked up where there was a no pick-up order. The despatcher sent her to the Grand Union, so she crawled along through the traffic, humming Christmas carols and pretending she didn't see all the people flagging.

By the time she came out of the Grand Union with the person who phoned, a man and a woman had walked across from Woodward's and were getting in the cab.

I'll call you another cab, Shannon told them.

Will it come soon?

No. It's Christmas. It probably won't come at all.

She got into the car to call a flag. The man from the Grand Union was a drunk with only one leg, hobbling along on crutches. When Shannon finished calling the flag, he still hadn't got into the car and Shannon saw that the woman was preventing him from getting in. She got out again and went to open the door for him.

I'm sorry, she said to the people. It's his cab. You'll have to wait.

The two looked at her appalled. They were rich and modly clothed and perfumed and manicured. The drunk was ragged and dirty and crippled.

But we're going to the Bayshore! the woman wailed.

I hope, Shannon said to the cripple, driving away, that you are about to spend your welfare cheque on booze the way you're supposed to.

I keep enough out for the rent. I always pay the rent first.

Shannon stopped at the liquor store and bought the two bottles of wine that he wanted, then carried them up some rickety steps at the broken-down rooming house where he lived. It would be several days before he had to face again the reality of

the awful place where he lived or the awfulness of having only
one leg.

It was her last trip of the day and she was tired of fighting
traffic and maniacs, but felt obliged to go see Gerald in case he
needed any money.

Gerald didn't need money. He had got a cheque to cover the
fare home from his mother, and a job offer from his father.

Good, Shannon said. Maybe you can regain your health. But
she felt depressed and betrayed and wished he hadn't chosen this
time to rejoin the decent citizenry.

She worked Christmas Day, and since Bradley was home,
didn't feel obliged to go upstairs for Christmas dinner. Evelyn
had saved a drumstick for her nevertheless, and the baby said if
Shannon came upstairs, she would sing for her.

My true love gave to me five gorun rings, the baby sang,
banging on the guitar she had received that morning.

Now you have to clap, she told them, and bowed politely and
modestly. She really enjoyed the game until the adults were sick
of clapping. Immediately she had a series of temper tantrums and
had to be put to bed.

What's the matter with her? Shannon asked Evelyn.

She hasn't ever gotten so much stuff at once before. She was
okay after the first present, but when she saw there was more she
got really confused and ran around tearing at things and
screamed that she wanted even more. She got this glazed look in
her eyes and just screamed about everything. Up till now, you
know, she only liked giving, and receiving gifts didn't mean
anything.

Well, that's the purpose of Christmas.

Fucking capitalist plot, Bradley said, pouring them all another
drink.

The baby screamed to be let out of bed, and screamed when
she was allowed out, and the whole thing lasted about three
hours. Shannon got drunk out of her mind and couldn't make it
to work the next morning, which cost her another $10 after she
had just finished paying the $40 for being ill in the fall.

January 1972

Shannon came within inches of being clobbered by a police car going through a stop sign at 40 mph, so she had two breakfasts and a lunch. Some mornings are like that. Every stop sign has a car speeding towards it; every parking lane contains drivers about to pull out without looking over their left shoulder; every parked car has a pedestrian crouched behind it, waiting to dash across the road. Her owner would be upset about the sheet, and having just acquired an owner (she had set a record at Purple Door for length of service without a steady owner), she shouldn't antagonize him. But what can you do on mornings like that?

Most of the time Shannon ate breakfast alone, savouring every mouthful of eggs and ham and brown toast and marmalade, and then lingering over coffee with the *Province*. There wasn't much to read in the *Province*, and it didn't usually last through breakfast, so she was forced to begin doing the crossword puzzle over coffee. She loved her lonely breakfasts and resented finding another driver in the restaurant. However, since she was having two breakfasts and Pete said he was having breakfast that morning, she joined him and some other drivers at the Black Angus. Most day drivers didn't take breaks during their nine-hour shift. They made more money than she did.

It was the usual kind of conversation with drivers. Shannon pretended she was reading the paper but she had already read it. She asked them not to make racist statements in her presence, so they started cutting up women and told her she didn't have any sense of humour. Shannon told them about being just missed by a cop car and all three of them agreed that there were mornings when all the cars on your right were about to change lanes without checking and all orange lights had someone speeding through them, and that on days like that it was best to park the car and go home. Shannon said her owner was unhappy about her low sheets, but they told her not to listen to him. He was trying to get all women day drivers because his cars had been smashed up a phenomenal number of times, and for a while, he would care less about low sheets than accidents.

Then I should just park the car. What will I say to the office?

Tell them you're sick. You don't look good. They'll believe you.

I've been fighting off the flu for a week, Shannon said. If I park the car, the bugs will think they have won and I'll get really sick.

Then they started telling her about all the accidents they had ever had. They seemed to have enjoyed all of them. It was the only way to deal with accidents since they were going to have them anyway, and so long as they weren't permanently crippled, it was just part of the job. They didn't talk about all the guys who lost their jobs over accidents. Everybody had accidents, but when you went before the Safety Committee, they acted as if it was a terrible sin you had personally invented.

The drivers also told Shannon another guy had been hit on the head the night before. Hold-ups always came in spurts, so there would be one every night for a week, and then none for months while drivers nervously gripped their tire irons and tried to persuade everyone to sit in front. The driver who had been hit on the head brought to six the number of Purple Door drivers in St. Paul's that week. One accident, two assaults, one stroke, one terminal cancer, one bleeding ulcer.

In the afternoon, Shannon felt feverish so she parked the car an hour early and went home. She hadn't had an accident after all, but she felt decidedly ill.

The baby had the flu too. Now that Shannon had a steady owner, she wouldn't have to pay for being sick; she would just lose wages, so she felt quite cheerful about it and told Evelyn she hoped the doctors never found a cure for the common cold because then how would the slaves of capitalism ever get any rest? Evelyn was upset because the baby had flu off and on all winter, and the doctors hadn't anything to suggest. She had dropped behind normal physical development again, and sniffled all the time, though she still made a remarkable amount of noise.

Bradley moved the baby's bed into Shannon's room, saying he was sick of listening to coughing and sick of wiping snotty noses and that he and Evelyn were going to watch TV and neck. But one or the other of them was downstairs every five minutes, checking to see how the invalids were. Shannon and the baby slept most of the first night and the first day. After that they were feeling better, but they plotted together and decided not to tell anyone so that they could be sick together a while longer.

Don't call me baby, the baby told Shannon.

Aren't you a baby any more?

I haven't been a baby for a long time.

What are you then?

A person.

A small person. Also an extraordinary person. Suppose I call you ESP, for extraordinary small person?

I'm not small. I'm big.

You are certainly bigger than you were before, but you're not as big as I am. Relatively Small Person, then.

Call me Bam Bam.

Bam Bam?

Yes. Like on TV.

Oh, Lord, have your recalcitrant parents been letting you watch that garbage? Didn't they warn you it would poison your brain?

Bradley said I was old enough to decide myself.

Cop-out. Your father is a cop-out.

No he's not. He's a construction worker.

He isn't that either. He's an unemployed bum.

You're a bum!

No, I'm not. I have a job. If you call what I have a job. Furthermore, you should be toilet-trained already.

Evelyn danced around and Bradley sang of the virtues of poo-poo and pee-pee in the potty. The baby learned the song immediately, but shunned the potty. She was learning to print and could spell everyone's name, but Evelyn was still washing diapers. Evelyn thought that her slow physical development was due to the large number of illnesses, but that the physical problems hadn't retarded her mental and emotional development.

The baby abandoned her own bed and brought her trucks and dolls and books and crayons into Shannon's bed. Evelyn brought down the Scrabble game, and Bradley the guitar.

It was a pleasant interlude of unreality, and Shannon remembered it hungrily for years afterwards.

February 1972

The dying year of the Social Credit government was accompanied by protest against the repressive labour legislation. In addition, strange events were beginning to occur among workers. Besides the move towards Canadian unions, women were becoming bolder. The waitresses at Smitty's Pancakes organized into a union. It was the Hotel and Restaurant Employees, which allowed two of the waitresses to be fired. This taught women both the virtues of organizing and the stupidity of traditional unions. Staff at UBC began organizing themselves also. At first they were undecided whether to join OTEU or CUPE, but contact with these unions convinced them they should begin the long and difficult struggle for an independent union.

The IBEW was on strike and Shannon wasn't sure what she should do when she got to the picket line. The woman from the Grosvenor was taking a cab because she was under the impression cabs would cross picket lines. Shannon didn't tell her otherwise, and when they got to the airport there was no picket line.

On the way back, she was sent to Park Drive. Three young women were going from there to the bus depot. They had arrived in town only the night before and knew no one. A guy had picked them up and taken them home, and there they had lost one of the girls. They thought she might already be at the bus depot. The fare was $2.95 and, between them, they had that much money, but then Shannon realized it was all the money they had and irritably gave it back to them.

She found an empty stand in front of the Georgia and read the paper. After a while a woman got in the cab, but it turned out she only wanted to change her boots. They were on the wrong feet and her feet hurt.

I'm four months pregnant, she told Shannon, and my husband will kill me if I don't have an abortion.

Do you want to have a baby?

Yes.

Then you could try welfare.

I already tried them and they turned me down. I'll try Indian Affairs next. It might not be deformed, it might be born alive.

You're a junkie? Shannon asked. The woman nodded. The baby will be all right if you eat good, Shannon told her. It'll just be born a junkie unless you get off it soon.

I will.

What are you doing in the meantime?

Just walking around. I have nowhere to go. Last night I heard he wasn't home so I went home to sleep, but then I set the house on fire. Not the house, just the couch. I was smoking and I musta been drunk. He'll kill me for sure now, if he finds out.

Then don't let him find you. Did you call the fire department?

Yes, I called them and then I left. Say, you wouldn't drive me to the Blue Eagle?

Okay. I don't seem to be doing anything else.

Thanks. I was in such a hurry to get away before my husband got home, I put my boots on the wrong feet and now my feet hurt.

At the Blue Eagle she asked Shannon again if there was a chance the baby might be alive, and Shannon assured her there was a very good chance.

Thanks. As long as there's a chance, I'll figure something out.

It had been a good move, because in zone one Shannon got two trips right away, though both were only jerks. The first one was a child, about 13 or 14, going to Campbell Avenue. As she was getting out, a syringe and needle fell out of her coat pocket. She was very young and did not know how to be a proper junkie yet.

The next passengers were going to Canadian Fishing. Shannon couldn't remember where it was and they said they didn't know either.

We're dumb Indians from Prince Rupert, that's why we don't know the way, one of them said.

I couldn't find Prince Rupert, Shannon told them, let alone anything in it. What does that make me?

A cab-driver.

The young man on the Lion's Gate bridge had been persuaded off by car 76 at 2 a.m. At 4 a.m., car 3 sighted him on the bridge again and called the police, who couldn't find the guy for a while. When they found him, they drove him to the south end again.

Just before 6 a.m., Shannon was taking a drunk couple to North Vancouver and saw the man on the bridge again. She told the despatcher, who muttered inaudibly because you couldn't swear on the radio. When she was coming back, the young man was leading a parade. He was walking purposefully north on the bridge, followed by two police cars flashing their red lights. It was all quite impressive, only there wasn't anywhere for the young man to go, no jobs to be had, and if he wasn't back the next night he would be back later.

Shannon got some coffee at the George II and when she came out, there was a man walking slowly down Denman, peering intently all around.

Have you seen a thousand dollar bill? he asked Shannon.

No, she said looking around, have you lost one?

No, but someone else might have and I'd be the first to find it.

No, you wouldn't. I'd find it first.

You would not. I'd find it first.

I get up earlier. I'd find it first.

Fucking taxi-drivers. All thieves.

After that, Shannon drove two longshoremen to work, and

that was a pleasant interlude in the morning. Workers always paid the fare and didn't hassle cab-drivers, assuming they were workers just like themselves.

The Queen of Sheba from Gastown was really named George, and was a tough guy who looked like a boxer. He had two servants who despised him, but who jumped whenever he gave them orders, which he did frequently in a nasty manner. He was paying their rent and they expected to get more than that out of him, and in return they had to run whenever he told them to run. The trio stopped at the bus depot and two other places where the Queen had his servants run errands for him, then they went back to the Metropole. There the Queen ordered the servant he called his husband to pay the fare which the man did but with the most pitiful protests. He also told the husband to give Shannon a tip, but the servant balked at that and got out of the cab. The Queen gave Shannon 50 cents. Here you are sweetie, he said, us girls have to stick together.

The next fare was drunk and wanted to give her $20. She refused but he kept insisting she must take it.

Then you have to do whatever I say, he pleaded. You have to. You'll be my cab-driver then. Just like a girl I had once.

Shannon leaned him against a tree at the West End address he had given her and tucked the $20 in his pocket. I want you to be my cab-driver, he said, just like a girl I had once.

In the afternoon, Shannon drove a teacher to the BCTF office. He was in town discussing what they should do about Social Credit's new law that put a ceiling on teachers' wages. The man told Shannon the teachers in Kamloops were really angry and that many who had previously supported Social Credit and voted for Gaglardi would not do so in the next election.

Teachers didn't mind the other anti-labour laws, Shannon said bitterly, because they thought they were better than workers. Teachers supported Gaglardi, though he hounded and drove people on welfare insane. Smash workers, stomp on the poor; that's all okay, but he shouldn't have touched the teachers.

The teacher didn't get mad or react in any way because he wasn't listening. Hardly anyone, and certainly never a lawyer or a teacher, listened to what cab-drivers had to say.

The drivers received their keys through a slot under a tiny, filthy window. They could barely see the people inside, and were thus intimidated into silence when office staff yelled at them through the greasy window. There had been a time when Shannon was very polite, and as friendly as the little hole permitted, to the office staff, and invariably cooperative with despatchers. But over the years she found that the office staff went out of their way to pick on drivers and would not explain anything. Drivers weren't even to know exactly how much commission they were making, and they couldn't find out if unemployment insurance or income tax was being paid on their behalf, and the office staff, if asked, would snarl through the greasy window and disappear. The office and despatch staff identified with the owners and treated the drivers like half-wild animals. Owners were allowed into the office and might talk to despatchers, so their relationship with the staff was that of normal people. Drivers were not allowed inside and could only communicate through the little slot below the greasy window. There didn't seem to be any reason for not making the window bigger, except to keep the drivers intimidated.

The driver ahead of Shannon had his ear to the window and his face turned towards her. Someone inside was yelling that he didn't work for Purple Door any more.

But why, the driver asked, why?

Go ask the manager.

Where do I find the manager?

You don't. He isn't here today.

But nobody told me. Why am I fired?

Fuck off.

The person on the other side of the window disappeared, and the man pounded on the wall but got no further reply. He leaned his head against the window for a minute and then turned and walked out past Shannon, his face expressionless, as if he was walking in his sleep.

Shannon got her keys and drove around for a while, then picked up a flag to zone one. She parked on the Balmoral and watched three people walking up Hastings. It took them half an hour to do the one block from Columbia to Main. By that time, Shannon had a fare. They were only going to the Ovaltine Cafe, and though Shannon pointed out it was only half a block walking and three blocks driving, they insisted they wanted a cab because it was raining.

When she dropped off the fare at the Ovaltine, the three people had arrived there, but it was obvious they weren't going much farther. A very drunk teenage girl was lying on the sidewalk while a drunk boy and sober girl were trying to carry her. Shannon helped the two put the girl in the cab, and then drove them to a broken-down building on Glen Drive, though they were embarrassed about not having any money.

I wasn't doing anything, Shannon said, and it's obvious you'd never make it walking.

But then there were two flights of rickety steps to go up. Why did poor people always have to deal with those treacherous stairs? Was it a commandment?

The boy, whose name was Jimmy, insisted he would carry the girl up the stairs. Halfway up, he dropped her, then lay on top of her, kissing her inert body. Shannon held onto both of them so they wouldn't tumble down and smash their heads on the concrete. She tried to pry Jimmy off, but he only moaned and kissed the wet body more passionately. She kicked him and he leaped up and shoved her aside, but she was holding on tight to a stair. She tried to push him down the stairs, but immediately regretted it and tried to explain to him reasonably that he was about to kill the girl. He didn't care. It was his girl friend and he could do what he wanted to her. He lay down on top of her again. Finally, by kicking him again, and with the help of the sober girl, they got the wet body to the top of the stairs and Shannon left them there.

She had to go around the block to get back onto Hastings, and when she got there, the sober girl was walking down the street.

Want a ride back to the Ovaltine? Shannon asked, and the girl did. She was a beautiful young woman of about 16. At 5 a.m. she had split with her old man and she had no money and nowhere to go. Shannon gave her $2 for breakfast.

I shouldn't have given it to her, she told Bradley. She should have to hustle that very first morning on the street.

She could get welfare and then get a job.

Are you out of your mind? She's an Indian. A really beautiful and healthy Indian woman. There are no jobs for her. Nobody in this democratic society would give her a job. Indian men can get longshoremen's jobs and a few other kinds of labourers jobs, but there aren't any choices for women. They're to fuck, and if she split with one man, she must be available to a whole bunch of them. There are no other choices. So I gave her $2.

Months later, Shannon was driving down Hastings with a passenger in the car when a woman tried to jump in front of it. Shannon stopped, and when the white man with the woman held her on the sidewalk, she drove slowly by. The woman was sobbing and trying to jump in the path of the car, and she was no longer beautiful but covered with the spit and vomit of Hastings Street, and it had only taken three months.

March 1972

The customs man was stuck with looking after the lady, and he didn't seem too happy about it. Her husband had left the ship in Latin America since he couldn't leave his business for four months, while she had continued around the world on the *Oriental Esmeralda*. She wasn't used to looking after herself, and was quite sure that if she didn't insist, she wouldn't be treated with the deference her husband's wife deserved.

The customs man put her in the back seat and talked with Shannon in front.

There must be a limousine, the lady interrupted.

There is, Shannon told her. I'll take you there as soon as we've taken this guy to Customs House.

That seemed to agitate her, and she got even more agitated when the man didn't get out of the car immediately at his destination, but told Shannon about their new quarters.

I want to go to the airport, she told Shannon.

Two bits more to the limousine, or 5 bucks to the airport, lady, Shannon said.

The lady was obviously not about to take the limousine, since it would involve carrying her own luggage, but Shannon was supposed to grovel and plead for the privilege of taking her to the airport.

Take me to the airport, she muttered.

The *Esmeralda* always docks at the cheapest and dirtiest dock, the lady whined. Awful. And it's a dirty ship. There's a lot to do – games and dances – but they don't keep it *clean*. You can tell them and tell them and they say yes but they never do it.

Who?

The Chinese. You can tell them and tell them and it's still dirty.

Where does the ship start from?

Taiwan. Then Vancouver. Los Angeles, through the Panama Canal to Key West in Florida, South America, Capetown and Durham in South Africa, Singapore, Taiwan, Kobe, and then back to Vancouver. Durham was marvellous. I really enjoyed Durham.

How come?

They're such *clean* places. Not very big, but *clean*.

Well, they've got enough people working for nothing.

And in Singapore it's a crime to throw a cigarette butt on the street.

What about Taiwan?

Taiwan was interesting. The interesting thing was seeing all those containers. There is a strike in the U.S., you know, on the docks, and those goods wait at all the ports of the world to be moved. The goods of the world come to the U.S., you know.

I know. All of them. (Lady, do you have to be such a stereotype?)

Have you ever been anywhere? she asked Shannon sympathetically.

Lady, I *am* somewhere.

I mean, somewhere else, like Los Angeles.

No, Shannon replied. (You can't disappoint them. You couldn't say, Lady, I've been around the world fourteen times and my brother is a movie director in Hollywood. It isn't nice. No tip, furthermore.)

You wouldn't like Los Angeles, the woman said comfortingly. It's a dirty city. And now all those hippies have come.

Where did they come from?

Who?

The hippies.

The lady looked confused. I don't know. They just come from all over. They're dirty.

Lady, those are somebody's children.

Oh, really? It was obvious she didn't believe it.

Do we get a prize for getting the most nickel tips?

Yeah, a nickel.

The drunk from the New World wasn't down yet, but four servants were running down the stairs with his belongings: a suitcase, a TV set, and two cases of beer.

John's coming down in a minute, they told Shannon.

Where is he going?

They didn't know. John had got drunk and was being kicked out of the New World for setting fire to his bed. He must have had a lot of money left, otherwise he wouldn't have had so many servants. Two of the servants, a woman and a young Indian man, left. Either they had got theirs already or weren't playing the game.

John came strolling out of the New World, carrying a coke, three bottles of wine in a paper bag, and a nearly empty bottle of vodka. One of the servants opened the door for him with a flourish, and John grandly seated himself in the back seat.

Have a heart, John, the servant whined. You don't need the rest of that bottle.

John sucked thoughtfully at his coke, then with many unnecessary motions, handed the vodka bottle to the servant.

Thank you, thank you, the servant said humbly, backing away until he was in the doorway of the New World, then disappearing into its depths. That left the man with the bandaged face, who spoke quietly and pleafully to John.

Give him two dollars, John said in a peremptory tone to Shannon.

Listen, Mac, she said, turning around to stare at him, ya wanna give him two dollars, do it yourself.

Give him two dollars, John said in the even tones of a man unaccustomed to disobedience.

Ya got the money to pay the fare? Shannon demanded. John had too much dignity to reply to such a question. He reached in his pocket, found $2 and some silver, and gave that to the servant, who touched his forehead respectfully and backed away around the corner.

The servant had forgotten to close John's door, and obviously John was above doing such things for himself. They sat there for a while, then Shannon got out and closed the door.

I'm going to the airport, John told her as a reward.

She started driving down Powell Street.

But first, John said a block later, I have to stop somewhere. Where?

The corner of Columbia and Hastings.

You mean the Broadway?

Yeah, the Broadway.

Some airport. Four blocks. Don't spill that coke, Shannon snarled.

It was too late. Coke was already running into the front from under the seat. At the light at Main, Shannon reached over the back seat, picked up the bottle, and smashed it into the side-walk. John didn't say anything.

At the Broadway, he told her to wait. In a few minutes he came out, told her it was okay, and disappeared inside again. Seemed he wasn't about to carry his own luggage. Shannon took the TV set and the two cases of beer in first. Then she went back out for the suitcase and the paper bag. The suitcase was a large one and she got tangled up with the door, but John wasn't about to help. He was filling out the register. Finally Shannon got un-tangled and put the suitcase and bag beside the rest of the stuff. Then she walked over and leaned against the counter beside John. He ignored her.

Gonna pay the fare, Mac?

How much?

$1.05.

The desk clerk watched them warily. John slowly pulled out a huge wad of bills, selected a $10 bill from it, and slid it along the counter towards Shannon.

Got anything smaller? she asked. I can't change that.

If she was a man, he would have beat her up. Women must be dealt with in other ways. He selected a $2 bill and slid that over.

I don't want any change, he said.

Shannon stuck the $2 bill in her pocket and slid the $10 bill back towards him.

He pushed it back again. I said I didn't want any change, he said, grinning at her for the first time.

The desk clerk seemed to be holding his breath. He and Shannon looked at each other for a moment, then Shannon stuck the ten dollar bill in her pocket and left without looking at the clerk again.

She paid the kid at the garage a dollar for paper towels and water to clean the coke from the floor, and found herself retching while cleaning. But it soon passed. Well, she said to herself, did I expect to wade through shit and come out clean?

April 29, 1972

Quang Tri was surrounded and within a few days the retreat began.

The inside Civic Workers were still on strike.

A woman jumped off the south end of the Granville Bridge at 8:20 a.m.

Donald Bates stalled on the Howe stand and couldn't get the trip he'd been sent on.

Oh well, you're too old anyhow, the despatcher said, and sent another car.

Where are ya, Donny? Marjie asked. I'll come and give you a jump.

There was a silence and muffled giggles and then Donald said proudly to the despatcher: Still think I'm too old?

A man left his key in Shannon's cab and she wasn't able to find him again to return it. He had told her he stole for a living.

It beats working, he said, mostly because I can't get a job. It beats welfare because then you don't feel sorry for yourself.

He asked Shannon the time and then discovered his watch was an hour slow.

Do you know why my watch is slow? he asked Shannon.

Because you forgot to change to Daylight Saving Time.

Nope.

You're an hour slow because you're an Indian.

That's why, he said, laughing so hard his stomach shook out of his jeans. Boy, you're sharp.

Yeah, Shannon said. I've seen everything and didn't like any of it.

He laughed some more.

A woman from St. Paul's asked Shannon the name of a good motel, but Shannon didn't know any. After much discussion she took the woman to the Downtowner Motel. On the way, the woman told her she was 53 years old and that her husband had left her some time ago. Now she wanted to start a new life, have a good time, get a job. She had started by getting a complete remake. Her nose had been bobbed, chin unsagged, face uplifted, breasts built up, fat cut away. Shannon thought how much a person would have to despise themselves to go through that kind of butchery.

Am I not beautiful? the woman asked.

Shannon looked at her in the mirror and smiled and said the lie the woman wanted to hear. The woman then pulled out some pictures of a beautiful motherly and human woman, and said that was what she looked like before. Now she only looked plastic and stiff and certainly no longer human, except for her pleading eyes.

A young man slept on the corner of Pender and Howe. Indian men ought not sleep in the financial district on a weekday afternoon, but this one was too drunk to know any better. Aspiring junior executives were embarrassed by him, so they flagged a passing cab and placed the young man in the back seat.

Has he got any money? Shannon asked.

Of course, one of the junior executives said, and hurried away in great embarrassment.

The young man slept in the back seat.

Dumb bastard, Shannon said. Don't you know your place? Imagine passing out in the financial district!

The man slept. He was a very handsome young man wearing a really neat purple shirt. Shannon shook him but he wouldn't wake up. Finally, in an extreme of frustration, she slapped him. He came awake and looked at her with bloodshot eyes.

Where do you live?

Richmond, he said and went back to sleep.

I'm not taking you to Richmond. When we get there you'll decide it should have been North Vancouver. Have you got any money? Whereabouts in Richmond?

The young man slept. Shannon shook him again but he wouldn't wake up.

No good drunken bastard, she yelled at him. Why don't you go to university and get a degree and be somebody? Why don't you get a job as a messenger boy and work your way up to plant chairman? Why don't you work at some stupid job for 45 years and retire on a pension? Why don't you drive a cab to pay your debts and then discover you're only getting deeper into debt?

The man slept.

Shannon drove to St. Paul's Emergency. She went in, flagged a passing intern, and asked him to help her get the man inside.

What's wrong with him? the intern asked.

He's drunk.

We don't take drunks.

What am I supposed to do with him then?

I don't know.

Come and look at him, Shannon said, seizing the intern by the arm. He's ever such a nice young man.

The intern allowed himself to be led. He pulled out the man's wallet, which was empty.

He's ever such a nice young man, Shannon said. He just doesn't know he shouldn't be drunk on a Thursday afternoon, nor that he shouldn't pass out in the financial district. What am I to do with him?

Oh well, the intern said. I guess he can sleep it off here.

Shannon and the intern carefully lifted the young man out of the car. He awoke long enough to kiss the doctor's cheek, then the two of them disappeared inside the hospital with their arms around each other.

Spring arrived in a burst of hope. A Vietnamese offensive began in April and won nearly all the countryside for the Vietnamese, so the Americans and their lackeys hid in the cities and were afraid to venture beyond those boundaries except in airplanes. In

May, Nixon went to Russia, just after mining the harbours of Vietnam. The Russians did not complain about the mining. Americans were pleased about this new friendship, though it wasn't in fact friendship, but a collusion of empires conspiring against their people. In return for precision manufactured goods, neither the Russians nor the Chinese were going to do anything about the escalation of the war against their Vietnamese comrades. There were pictures of Mao and Chou, smiling, shaking Nixon's hand.

Soon after the presidential primaries began, Wallace was shot, leaving the racists and fascists with no one to vote for but Nixon, which was indeed a blessing for him.

Elsewhere, 25 people were shot by terrorists in Tel Aviv airport. It was presumably on behalf of the disinherited Palestinians, except that most of the people killed had been Puerto Ricans making a pilgrimage to the holy land.

In Quebec, events were leading towards a general strike.

In B.C., the fallers were still out on strike. Wire Rope workers were on strike. The Civic Workers strike in Vancouver began on April 27. City Council voted itself a substantial raise and then the mayor went to London.

Bradley demanded that Shannon cease being depressed and talk more. Bradley had a job as a casual longshoreman now, which meant he didn't have to leave town and he didn't have to work very often, so he was fairly satisfied with the world and asked Shannon why she couldn't be happy once in a while. But Shannon asked, what's to be happy about? Evelyn was taking night school courses and was full of enthusiasm about the people and books involved, and she asked Shannon why she wasn't happy. What's to be happy about? Shannon asked.

The baby stopped getting colds for a while and got toilet trained and learned to ride a bike and made friends with the boy next door and also asked Shannon why she wasn't happy, to which Shannon replied: What's to be happy about?

It was a warm and sunny spring, so the baby didn't visit Shannon's dark basement nearly so often, preferring to ride her bike or nag the boy next door.

Gerald sent a cheque for $100 and wrote that the job for his father hadn't worked out, but he had worked long enough to collect unemployment insurance and preferred being an unemployed worker to being a bum. He was, he assured her, eating lots of yogurt.

There was a man lying on the sidewalk by the West Hotel, and Shannon stopped to see if he was dead. He wasn't, so she picked up the mike to tell the despatcher to inform the police. But a terrible inertia took hold of her, so she just sat there for a while and then drove away. The police might take him to jail. Or they might call an ambulance to take him to a hospital where he would be tortured by useless treatments. There wasn't anywhere he could be taken where he would be helped. Let him sleep, then. Just for a short time he would be left in peace on the sun-drenched sidewalk.

Are there many women drivers?

Yeah. A lot. It wasn't true, but Shannon always said that because it upset people so much.

But you're not allowed to drive nights? they asked pleadingly.

No.

They relaxed. Women were still in their place and all was right with the world.

Shannon stared with sleep-glazed eyes at the people walking down Columbia. Ragged. Drunk. Doped. Mean. Even the women would turn on you with horrible viciousness, like a trapped rat, because they hurt all over.

A neatly pressed man stopped by the car.

Say, I used to be a driver myself. I don't suppose you'd give me a quarter.

Shannon gave him a dollar, as she did to anyone who said he'd been a driver.

Why aren't you driving now? she asked.

Court. I drove for Sahara. I figgered if you're going to drive cab you might as well make money at it. The guy says you can't drive for Sahara if you don't bootleg, and I didn't mind. Thought it would be good money. There's money in bootlegging. I wasn't going to try living on a driver's pay. That's for suckers.

Did you make any money?

Well, they caught me. We can't allow a man like you to drive a taxi, the judge says to me.

Did you say we couldn't allow a man like him to sit in judgment over us?

Naw. I didn't say anything. Just pleaded guilty. I was caught.

Couldn't you have told them about Sahara and how you can't drive for them unless you bootleg?

I couldn't, I was caught. I'm still walking around and I'm not crippled. Gangsters, you know.

But surely they know Sahara is a bootleg and pimp joint.

Surely. You just don't get caught.

Couldn't you get another job?

I've applied at 25 or more different places. Last week, I went up to 41st and Oak, where they hire the bus drivers, you know. I filled out the application form and then when I was handing it in, the guy says, do you have a criminal record? What can you say? I just turned and walked out.

Does it matter if bus-drivers ever bootlegged?

I don't know. What can you say? They caught me.

April 1972

It was raining in the morning.

In Vietnam, the offensive was proceeding apace and victory seemed very near at hand.

In Quebec, the unions formed a Common Front and, among other demands, were asking for a minimum wage of $100 a week for everyone. This affected women mostly, since few male workers earned less than that amount. Nurse's aides, nurses, and others all went to jail for defying anti-labour laws. When the union leaders were jailed, nearly all workers stopped working and a general strike was imminent. Workers who didn't strike occupied their places of work with great success.

Shannon asked a few drivers what they thought about it, and

was depressed by the lack of response. The passengers were about the same. Passengers are always the same.

At 612 Davie, Shannon told the despatcher mournfully, some people looked at me and then locked the door.

I don't blame them, he replied. You're first in town again.

A Chartreuse driver came along and pounded on the door of 612 Davie. They've locked up, Shannon told her.

They can't. I've got a pre-date. She pounded on the door again.

Two drunk men came staggering by. Shannon got back in the car to read the paper. She could hear the men talking to the Chartreuse driver. The handsome one wanted her to drive them to New West for a flat $5, but she said all fares had to go on the meter. It was a long and boring argument. The other one came around to Shannon's window and asked her the same question, to which she gave the same answer and continued reading the paper. He said please about 39 times. The Chartreuse driver radioed in to ask if it was okay to drive them to New West for $5. Shannon looked the guys over and they were cute, the kind of cute that figures the world owes them a living.

Have you got any money? she asked them.

Sure.

Where?

In my room.

You don't have any here? Where is your room?

Nanaimo and Hastings.

But you wanted to go to New West.

He lives there.

So you'd have to stop along the way to get money?

Guess so.

And you still want to go for $5. You don't want much, do you? Here, take a bus. She gave him a dollar.

Thanks, he said. I'll see you next Friday about repaying it.

Fat chance, Shannon sneered and returned to the paper.

The Chartreuse driver had returned now, and they asked her again about going to New West for $5. Shannon told her they didn't have any money.

None? She looked at them disbelievingly and they both hung their heads. Why don't you give them bus fare and drive them to the bus depot?

I've already given them $1. You drive them to the depot.

They got in the Chartreuse cab and drove away. Shannon asked the despatcher irritably if he had forgotten her, and he said no, there weren't any trips. The passenger door opened and the handsomer drunk got in. Shannon looked around but couldn't see the Chartreuse taxi anywhere.

Where the hell did you come from? she asked.

I came back.

Obviously.

I've fallen in love with you.

Sure, every second drunk falls in love with me. That's why they all try to rip me off.

But I *have*. I really dig you.

Shit, Shannon said. What do you know about me?

Are you married?

That's all that's important, eh? she said bitterly.

I'm in love with you.

Get out of my car.

His face crumpled. Shannon couldn't stand men crying and didn't know what to do. Look, he sobbed, see, I'm a queer and I don't wanna be and I thought ...

Finally the despatcher was calling and he read out an address, to which Shannon replied: Roger.

Didn't you hear me? the man beside her asked.

Yeah, you got problems. Well, I've got a trip. You'll have to get out of the car.

But ... See, I screw guys and I never ... I thought ...

Look, Mac, I'm sure you've got really serious problems. I'm equally sure I can't do anything about them. I've got a trip now and you gotta get out.

Can't you take me to the bus depot?

No. You had a ride and you didn't take it.

How am I gonna get to the bus depot?

I guess you'll have to walk. It's not very far.

Don't you care?

No. You're like all the rest of em, Mac. Stand there whining and looking helpless and saying I love you, and I'm supposed to take you in my arms and whisper there, there, don't cry, Mama will take care of you, and not worry you about the babies or anything like that.

Guess I'll have to walk, he said.

May 1972

A second Fred Quilt inquest had been ordered.

The NLF were winning all over Vietnam.

Quebec workers took over a town and closed down all large businesses as well as taking over the radio and TV stations.

Heading for the Abbott stand, Shannon was flagged by two men on the Carrall stand. They were going to a West End apartment.

The men were sober drunks, painfully clean. They told Shannon someone from the apartment had called Central City Mission for two men to move stuff from the 16th floor to the 14th floor. She asked them how much they would be paid and they said they hadn't thought it was nice to ask, so Shannon didn't talk to them any more.

They're tearing down Pigeon Park, one of them said to the other.

Yeah, the merchants are complaining.

They shouldn't call it Pigeon Park, they should call it Indian Park. I'm scared to walk down that side of the sheet. It isn't nice. They brought it on themselves. Sitting there, talking dirty. People don't like to hear that kind of stuff. It isn't nice.

The Americans are taking a beating.

Yeah.

They had no business being there.

I read that 99% of the soldiers are Negroes. If they pull out, it'll be a real problem. What to do with the Negro. There's so many of them again. In World War Two, the first strike in Europe was all Negroes and they got killed. But there's a lot of them again. Dunno what they'll do with them if they have to pull out of Vietnam.

The next trip was from the West End to Kits. It was a hippie woman moving a whole bunch of stuff. Shannon was already tired and the stuff was heavy, but the woman looked poor so Shannon didn't tell her there was an extra charge for moving. When the woman started talking, Shannon was sorry she hadn't charged her extra.

The woman said boys should look like boys and girls should look like girls, because then they would have an identity. In this case, identity was completely derived from other people's opinion. But she also said that women were oppressed only if they thought they were, and they should have an identity which transcended sexism and poverty. Now identity had suddenly become something derived from inner strength and had nothing to do with people's opinion.

Muttering about stupid bigots and stupid drunks, Shannon delivered a very old and fragile man to the Seymour Medical Clinic, then she got a trip from the zone to the Pennsylvania.

The next call was to the Grand Union. It was a drunk with cuts all over his face. Shannon asked if he had any money, which incensed him. It turned out he had been refused service at the Grand Union, the fucking bastards, though he had money, and he'd never go back there again, that would teach them, they didn't know who they were dealing with.

They know who they're dealing with all right, Shannon said, and they know enough not to serve broken-down drunks.

I'm not. You haven't been anywhere and don't know anything. I'm a really big man. I used to be a miner.

Well, you're not a miner now, but a broken-down drunk.

Aw, you can't even drive. Fucking bitch.

I don't beg for money, Shannon said.

I don't beg!

Broken-down drunks have money only if they begged it.

He was my friend, and he gave it to me! I don't beg, I'm a big man. Fucking bitch. I'll kill them fuckers. I can beat up anybody. Show me anybody and I can beat them up.

Shut up.

See that guy walking down the street there. Must be six feet. I can beat him up.

Shut up.

Hey, there's a guy from my home town. I can beat him up. Beat em to a pulp.

They were at the address on Hamilton he had given her. It don't look like much from the outside, the drunk said, but I got all sorts of things inside. *Lots* of *things*. I'm a big man. I can beat up anybody.

You couldn't beat up a cat, even. You're a broken-down drunk living in a condemned house and there isn't anything inside it.

There is so. *Things*. Lots of things. I can beat up anybody.

You can't.

Well, he said, getting out of the car. At least I'm going to beat the shit out of my wife.

After that there were mostly brown envelopes to deliver from one office to another. Traffic was heavy and Shannon had to keep a tight hold on herself to keep from screaming. And people kept asking if there were many women drivers, as if their world would fall to pieces if women weren't still in their place.

May 1972

I don't mind carrying luggage, but carrying passengers is a bit much.

Keep it up and maybe you'll get a job as a swamper on an ambulance.

Mildred.

What?

I'm tired of saying "Roger." Women should get equal time.
Oh. Mildred.

To prevent people from asking whether or not she was married, Shannon conducted a survey among her passengers to see
what they thought of the Civic Workers' strike. She had hoped
that the example of workers in Quebec taking control for even
such a short time would inspire workers elsewhere, but this
didn't seem to be the case. She found one day that 90% of her
passengers disapproved of the strike. They thought that the boss
was most qualified to decide whether a worker was good and how
much that worker should be paid. Although her passengers were
hardly representative, it didn't appear there was about to be a
socialist revolution.

One of those who had class consciousness was just barely able
to stand up in front of the Broadway Hotel, and was holding his
pants, which he informed her were "broken." He was a seaman,
he also told her. The night before, the police had arrested him
for being drunk, which he freely admitted he was. Neither did he
object to being taken to jail. However, there was a picket line in
front of the jail and he was a seaman who had never crossed a
picket line and wasn't about to start now. He weighed 270
pounds and the police had to carry him across the picket line,
with him struggling and apologizing to the civic workers all the
way. In the process, he got a bit bruised up and his pants had got
broken. At his apartment, he asked Shannon to stop by the back
door because if the neighbours saw him with broken pants, they
would immediately assume she had raped him, and he didn't
wish to tarnish her undoubtedly impeccable reputation.

It was an otherwise boring day, but the incident put Shannon
in a good mood, so she even talked to the young man who was
manager in a garment factory. The garment workers were paid
according to how much they sewed. Chinese and East Indian
women took five days to train, other kinds of Canadian women
took two weeks. The young man, who was a university student,
reckoned it was because Chinese and Indian women were more
single-minded and knew their place, and Shannon remarked
that what he was basically saying was they had been terrorized.

She also asked what his qualifications for being manager were, and had he ever sewed garments himself and been paid for how fast he sewed? He said of course not, but he was a man and a university student.

Things are changing, Shannon wrote to Gerald, but they are not changing fast enough. There are independent unions springing up all over. People have suddenly gone nationalist again, only it doesn't appear to be Americans they're objecting to as much as the unions' habit of being determinedly ineffective. And some waitresses are organizing, for chrissake. Waitresses. Isn't that wonderful? Some women have formed a union of their own because they object to male bureaucrats, but unlike other groups, they don't think the answer is to replace them with female bureaucrats.

But unemployment is up to 10% and the number of suicides and murders is increasing. Dope is now also a problem with children as well as with adults. The city is changing. There's a new porno place opening every month and the pimp joints Jack Wasserman likes so much are becoming much more overt. Sex, they tell me, is the hottest selling commodity on the market. Racism is acceptable as ordinary dinner table conversation. The scene at Davie and Granville has changed, and now prostitutes walk the street by the dozens without fear of apprehension, and dope is sold more or less openly. There is still the Columbia and Hastings scene, but only the wreckage is left there; the smart young lumpens have moved the scene of their businesses to Davie and Granville. That's because Gastown took away some space. Gastown has grown larger, and more genuine old-fashioned rip-off places are springing up all over. There are more beggars on the streets. People think colourfully ragged young men playing a guitar are romantic, but they are beggars and nothing more, and it's cold and hunger that makes them smile. I drove a young man to the bridge the other day, and he didn't even tip. Well, all that is nothing to be surprised about, being symptoms of disintegrating capitalism.

I won't go, Shannon said. I'd have to buy stockings.

I've got some panti-hose I'll give you. A belated Christmas gift, like. You always wanted to work in a library.

I did not. I only said of all women's jobs maybe working in a library was least bad.

How about being a professor or the head of a government department?

Those are for middle-class persons. They have some choices. I'm talking about us and there are no good jobs for us.

You have to go, Evelyn said. I made an appointment for you, saying, of course, that I was you. Maybe you can organize a union or something.

I won't go. Stockings itch. If I could organize unions, I'd get the drivers to form a union.

These are panti-hose, not stockings.

Panti-hose, shmanty-hose. They still itch. I don't have any shoes either.

You do so. You bought some for your last interview – how long ago was that?

Oh yeah, I forgot, I'm not going.

But she nearly always eventually did what Evelyn told her. She went and was interviewed and didn't speak to Evelyn for a week.

He said I was overqualified, she finally told her. I couldn't believe it. Because you'd said I'd worked in a library before, and my two years of university and that other office job I did. The one I quit. You should never quit jobs. I said, look man, it's either being a library assistant or a cab-driver – aren't I overqualified to drive a cab? Never again, boy, never again.

What are you going to do then?

Dunno. I'm making more money now.

You could make as much being a waitress.

Not quite, I don't think. Anyway, my feet would hurt.

Your fallen arches, Evelyn laughed.

Fallen arches aren't funny. You wouldn't find it so fucking funny if your feet hurt.

I'm sorry. But you could get another job.

Maybe. I'm not going to though. The guy at Canada Manpower a long time ago said to write a resumé and apply just everywhere and figure on about six weeks of job-hunting. When we were young, there wasn't such a thing, was there? You just went and got a job. Now you keep walking from one place to another for six weeks. I've stopped believing anyone would hire me. They'd be crazy, you know, crazy to hire me. Why would anyone give *me* a job? You know?

Other people get jobs.

I know. It's all so mysterious. Evelyn, I don't mind. I should be doing something more. Bradley thinks we should save the world. I don't know how. I don't know what to do. I'm proud of the fact that I can survive.

Do you like Bradley?

No. What's that got to do with it?

Nothing. Why don't you like him?

He's innocent. Nobody living in the jaws of the capitalist monster should be so innocent. Gerald at least learned it was a jungle, even if he learned nothing else. Of course I like Bradley. Who wouldn't? But he says we're responsible for the empire. I'm not. We don't have the power to change anything. So we sit in our prisons, flailing ourselves for comfort.

Bullshit. If you had another job, you'd have a different philosophy.

Quite. As Marx said. But I like driving cab. Receptionists, sales clerks, waitresses – they all have to look pleasant all the time. I can snarl if I want. There ain't too many women who can do that. Maybe garment workers are allowed to snarl at their sewing machines. But women mostly have to look pleasant when they're fucking miserable, and smile when they're angry. It's a big deal. The city is mine, too. The city belongs to those who know it. There's an arrogance that goes with being a taxi driver. You don't give a fuck about anything, and it's been years since I was surprised by anything. We don't, none of us, have very many choices. We can rebel. Organize, when there's a chance. Talk. But it's all madness. In the end, all we can choose is our kind of madness. If we're strong. I'm strong.

May 1972

The girl was thin and undernourished, yet possessed a strange kind of childish beauty. She was standing beside the Blackstone Hotel shivering in the pre-dawn cold. A police car drove by and the girl immediately went to the phone booth and pretended to dial a number. When the car passed, she returned again to her cold vigil beside the Blackstone. Prostitutes should be gay and garish and aging like they are in the movies, not this youthful skinniness, shivering in the pre-dawn chill. Finally a man came along, rich and self-satisfied looking. He walked by, and the girl straightened and stopped shivering. He came back and there was a short conversation, with the girl leaning forward and smiling at him. It appeared they couldn't understand one another, because the girl started using sign language and assured him unmistakably that he could indeed fuck her and it would only cost him five dollars. The man held up two fingers and she got a bit distraught, repeating the five fingers, but he stubbornly insisted on two. It all came clear when he held up both hands and then two fingers. With great relief, the girl led him over to the cab and gave Shannon a West End address.

Then Shannon got a couple of no loads, which irritated the hell out of her but amused the despatcher. They saw who was coming, he said. When drivers and despatchers insulted you, it showed they really liked you. Shannon would rather they

showed their affection for her and for each other with compli-
ments rather than insults, but then they wouldn't be taxi-
drivers, would they?

The proper day began and she spent most of the morning
delivering mail bags and parcels and brown envelopes. She also
drove Mr. de Crecy, and Mr. de Crecy chose Bernadette Devlin
as his text that morning. He was much more indignant about her
illegitimate baby than about her revolutionary activities, and
expressed amazement that she could get herself pregnant when
she was so ugly.

Just at the light at Broadway and Granville, Shannon
remembered what she had meant to tell Mr. de Crecy weeks
before. In the middle of his tirade about Bernadette Devlin, she
turned to him and said: Communism will be much better with
just us women and children here anyway.

He stopped talking and looked at her as if she had just lost her
mind. She reminded him that weeks before, he had claimed
Canadians would never be communists and that they would fight
to the last *man* to oppose it. Now at the red light at Broadway
and Granville, she had thought of the answer to that one, which
was that communism would be much better with just women and
children here. Mr. de Crecy looked at her in amazement and
then continued to tell her how it was illegal for women to get
pregnant without permission.

In the afternoon, she drove a couple from Osler Street to the
airport. Aging swingers is what they were, on the edge of the
ruling class, like Mr. de Crecy, who was a senior partner in a big
law firm. These people were a different type. Mean from years of
drinking. Mean from years of cursing each other like navvies in
private, and being polite with only sarcastic overtones in public.
Seething with chronic mean. They didn't want to talk to each
other because then they would start screaming, so they both
directed questions at Shannon which she only answered with
grunts.

You're not allowed to work nights, are you. You must have
many experiences. Your husband shouldn't let you do this. You

must make a lot of money. It's a nice day. Cops are nice to cabbies. They are not, Shannon said, turning around and speaking audibly for the first time. She was driving over the Oak Street bridge at 50 mph and it always totally unnerved people if she turned around and stared at them while doing that in three lanes of traffic. They are so, the woman screamed, they are so, they are so, they are so, don't argue with me or I won't tip, all cabbies are liars, they are so, they are so.

Just before quitting time, Shannon was driving by her house, so she stopped and asked the baby if she wanted to come for a free ride in a taxi. The baby did, so Shannon drove her down to the gas station and the baby watched the gassing up and cashing in process. Normally she was an awful loudmouth, but with all those drivers around, she clung to Shannon's leg with her thumb in her mouth. Shannon felt sympathetic and wished there was a leg large enough for her to cling to.

June 1972

Early in the morning, Shannon almost ran over a man lying on Cordova. She stopped to see if he was dead. His colour was okay and his heartbeat strong and steady, but he was emaciated and unconscious and had a strong smell of alcohol. Shannon lifted him carefully onto the sidewalk so he wouldn't get run over. She drove around for a while and finally saw two men and two women, all wearing buckskin jackets, walking down Hastings. She parked the car and ran across the street towards them.

Do you have a place to sleep? she asked.

The four people glanced at each other and started walking around her.

Wait, she said, I'm sorry for . . . please. There's a man lying on Cordova and I don't know what to do.

Is he an Indian? one of the men asked.

Yes. That's why. See, if I call the cops they'll kick him around because that's what they're paid to do. I don't know what to do. He looks like he hasn't eaten right for a long time.

Okay, we'll look after him.

I'll take you there. It's just a block – there, on Cordova.

That's okay. We'll take care of it.

Thanks. See, I never know what to do . . .

Sure, sure, the man said patronizingly and then all four of them hurried off towards Cordova.

The Civic Workers strike was finally settled.

A woman going to the airport wanted to know if there was a flat rate, and Shannon told her everything had to go on the meter. The woman said the fares were really too high and that there should be a flat rate. Shannon agreed the fares were too high, but couldn't see how a flat rate would make any difference. The woman said it only cost 50 pesos to the airport in Mexico.

The cost of living must be lower there.

No, it's the same as here, it's just the wages that are lower.

People starve then.

No, they don't. I got a real education over there. I don't know how they manage it, but they're happy. The taxi drivers smile at you.

Shannon stared at her in the mirror with surly hatred. They have to smile, she said, since what little income they do get depends on asslicking the tourists. And if you've got an education on how to be happy though poor, why don't you give me all your money and try it?

The woman would not speak to Shannon again, preferring to sit back and daydream of places where servants were servile instead of surly.

July 1972

Both Shannon and the car were gripped with sweat and inertia. The car wouldn't start on the Bayshore and Shannon was too hot to do anything about it, so she just sat there with the hood up and eventually the car started.

Early in the morning before the sun came up, when it was still cool, Shannon had been sent to Chinatown. The couple were only going half a block, but gave Shannon a dollar for watching them go in the door. She thought it most strange, but later Tom Hadley told her a man had been stabbed on Pender Street the night before.

Still early in the morning, Shannon was sent for a pre-date in the West End. She waited 17 minutes and turned on the meter for the last ten. When the man came out and saw that the meter was on, he complained about being ripped off. Shannon told him to find another cab, but he had to pay the waiting time first. He said he took a cab regularly to the airport and nobody had ever charged him for waiting time, so Shannon said he had been ripping off the drivers.

They drove towards the airport in silence. At the light at 70th and Oak, Shannon heard Tom Hadley saying something about calling the police because of trucks weaving over the bridge. She didn't get it straight. In the meantime, the light changed and she started driving over the Oak Street bridge.

There's two of them, Tom said on the radio, and they're weaving all over the bridge and one of them just went up on the sidewalk.

Okay, the despatcher said, I'm calling the police. Can you follow them?

Then Shannon saw them and it was too late to do anything. Just over the hump they came, two monstrously huge garbage trucks, one on each side of the road. Going between them would be suicidal. The driver of the truck coming at her was slumped over the wheel, and she didn't think blowing the horn would do any good. She pulled over as close as she could to the sidewalk and stopped, watching the monster approaching and cursing with every curse she knew. The truck passed by with about two inches to spare.

Shannon took a deep breath, put the car in gear, and continued towards the airport.

They're gonna kill somebody, she told the despatcher. Then

turning to her passenger, she said: I have to take that kind of shit, too, besides being ripped off and hassled by self-righteous passengers. He looked very pale and said he was sorry. At the airport he apologized again and gave her a $1 tip as if that would make everything all right.

After the sun came up, there was a long line-up of ragged men on Cordova Street, waiting patiently for food. Every day there was a line-up, but it seemed to be growing longer, or maybe, exposed to the glaring cruelty of the sun, it just seemed longer. All over Oppenheimer Park, men took this sunny opportunity to sleep.

A man vomited on the corner of Carrall and Hastings. At the bus stop, a ragged mother and five ragged children waited for a bus.

Later in the day, a broken-down hippie got in the cab at the bus depot and gave her a Kitsilano address. She went over the Cambie Bridge and down 4th Avenue and he started yelling that it would have been faster down Granville. She only charged him $1.25 for what should have been over $2.00 because he looked so broken down. It's okay to rip off cab-drivers, but it isn't okay for drivers to rip off passengers. Those are the rules.

The Bathtub Race was on. Thousands of people thronged Kitsilano Beach to watch the bathtubs come in. Every one of them brought a car, so the six blocks or so were impassable for anyone but a determined taxi-driver. Shannon got a couple of trips from there before the strain wore her down.

It was hot all summer. The combination of heat and fatigue and carbon monoxide made Shannon more sluggish and surly than before, so now the baby avoided her and wouldn't even come for any more taxi rides.

The man from 365 Cordova was going to the Downtowner. Shannon didn't remember where it was, but he said Thurlow and

Pender so she thought she would go down Pender Street. Hastings was impossible. Water Street jammed, and Dunsmuir wicked. But Pender was also jammed up.

Darling, the man had said, holding out his arms when he got into the cab.

Shannon recoiled in disgust. Keep your hands to yourself, Mac.

Darling what's wrong?

Don't call me darling.

Sweetheart.

Don't call me sweetheart, honey, baby or chick.

Are you married? he asked.

None of your business.

How do I know what to call you then?

You don't have to call me anything. We're just going from here to the Downtowner and then I'll never see you again, thank god, and you don't have to call me anything. We're not friends or relatives and I'm only stuck with you for a few minutes.

Christ, he muttered.

On Pender there were two lanes, but one was not moving because 99 was loading at the Niagara. Shannon was on the inside lane, inching forward slowly, furious at the traffic which would prevent her from getting rid of this sonofabitch very soon. The car behind 99 was trying to get into the inside lane and would have cut Shannon off, but she kept moving forward and wouldn't let the guy in. He did the finger at her and she stared at him while he frothed. About then, 99's passengers were in the car, but there was still a truck in front of him blocking the lane. Shannon let him in front of her and acknowledged his thanks with a smile. At which time the driver beside her, to whom she hadn't been so polite, went positively hysterical and screamed all kinds of swear words, and she was a bit worried he was going to get out and try to hit her. But she just yelled "go fuck yourself" and waited for the traffic to move.

Her passenger watched all this with amazement. You, he said, are the most unpleasant person I have ever met.

This pleased Shannon no end. A jerk like him must have met

a great many unpleasant people in his life. I'm pleasant to pleasant people, Shannon told him.

Am I not pleasant?

No.

What did I do wrong?

Unpleasantness comes so naturally to you, you're not even aware of it?

What did I do wrong?

Look, I'm no social worker nor any kind of reformist. I can't be bothered with people like you. Just let me ask you this: Do you think women are people?

Women are women. Vive le difference.

Shannon shrugged. See?

When you are so unpleasant, the man said, how do you expect to get any tips?

Shannon studied him while moving slowly forward down Pender Street. In spite of the traffic jam, the fare to the Downtowner would be only about $1.25, so the largest tip he would give would be two bits.

Tell you what, she said at last, I'll give you *four* bits if you smile real nice and tell me you're sorry.

What?

Well, that's what you're telling me to do.

No, it's not.

Okay, then, 75 cents.

There's not enough money in the world to buy me.

You better sell for 75 cents because it's the highest offer you'll ever get.

Shannon couldn't find a stand after that and the traffic was bad all over and nobody flagged her down. Eventually she ended up on the Davie stand, demoralized and thinking the day would never end. A man came out of the Blackstone and got in the car beside her. He gave her the address and she repeated it back and then he looked at her in shock the way they all do. Jesus Christ, a woman.

This one leaned over and stared at her face from six inches

away, and she thought how nice he would look with blood running down his face.

Jesus Christ, a woman.

Fuck off, she snarled, this isn't a zoo.

I'm sorry. It's just that you don't see many women drivers.

Fucking right you don't, when you treat them like animals.

I'm sorry, he said, leaning back. I didn't mean to insult you.

They never do, Shannon said, driving down Granville. They never do. It just never occurs to them we're people and not zoo animals to be stared at, and that we have feelings and don't like being prodded and mauled by thirty different guys in one day.

I'm sorry, he said again. You don't see many women drivers. I had another woman driver once drive me from the airport. Was it you?

We don't pick up at the airport.

But it was a woman who looked like you.

All women look the same.

She talked to me, this woman, who was a socialist. I called your cab company and asked what her name was. She is the most fascinating woman I have ever met in my whole life, I said, and I must find her again. They claimed they never gave out names or addresses. Was it you?

No. But Shannon remembered talking to him. It was when she still found ideas fascinating. But ... what she had inspired him to was not revolution, but sex. She felt sick and used and futile.

What did she talk to you about? she asked.

I don't remember. Everything. She was fascinating. It was you, wasn't it?

I don't remember you. We're not allowed to pick up at the airport. And look, Mac, women are people you know, and you can't treat them as if they were monkeys in a cage.

I think she said that.

Well, you didn't learn much, did you?

It was you. I know it was you.

We're at your address, Mac.

He stared at her, refusing to believe he was going to lose her again. Shannon stared back, hatred in her eyes, thinking again how nice he would look with blood running down his face. Then he threw a five dollar bill on the seat and got out. Shannon fumbled in her wallet for change, but he was gone and only the bill still lay on the seat. She wadded the bill into a lump and threw it after him.

After a while, she got out, uncrumpled the bill, and put it in her wallet. Then she booked into the West End.

July 1972

It was warm even in the early morning dark in the middle of summer. As the hot weather continued, sunrises became more and more fantastic due to heavy pollution being stained scarlet by the morning sun. It was quiet in the early morning. Later the roar of the traffic set up a steady din, but that early there was only the birds' singing.

Chinese women sat on street corners waiting for the trucks.

On the sidewalk on Powell, a group of kids were passing around a plastic bag.

A dead cat on Water Street.

There was a girl stumbling down Dunsmuir. A guy asked Shannon if she would give him a penny. He had given the girl all the money he had, which was 24 cents, so that she could take the bus, but it still wasn't enough. Shannon gave him a quarter to give the girl, but refrained from telling him it would be another hour before the buses started running.

A nurse went to work. A waitress went to work. A hooker went home. Two longshoremen went to work. Why is it that women work crazy shifts more often than men?

Morning rush hour. Shannon could ever only stand half of it, and for the other half she would park the car and go for breakfast.

Then jerks from one building to another. At least they didn't talk, these men in mod suits carrying briefcases. They came in pairs most often, and talked earnestly to each other in the back.

Unfortunately, if they were going some distance, they talked. One was going to the airport, and for good tips you had to be nice to them. He sat in front, his arm carelessly thrown along the back of the seat so that he almost touched Shannon's shoulder. He was handsome and dressed in the mod clothing that accentuated men's sexual attributes. Shannon felt kind of sick, but she had long since accepted the pain in her abdomen, along with her constant fatigue, as a normal part of life.

The man worked for the Royal Bank and was the manager of 91 branch managers. It was a good trip, so Shannon couldn't ask him about the bank's overseas investments nor about Canada's role as a mini-imperialist through its banks. She knew anyway what he would say, which was that Canadian investors deserved a safe investment and that it didn't matter if this was at the expense of the people of the Caribbean.

He asked Shannon if she was married and then told her women shouldn't drive cab. She said there weren't any decent jobs for women. He said there were and that there was no discrimination against women because he personally didn't discriminate against women. Of the 91 branch managers, however, none were women. He had previously had women managers, and he often promoted women in the lower ranks.

I treat my women employees just the same as the men. I say to them: Honey, if you work hard you can go places.

Honey? Do you call your men honey?

You know what I mean.

Yes. That there are no women managers and that you think of women primarily as sex objects.

But he didn't, he really didn't, and he was modly attired and handsome and his arm rested carelessly on the back of the seat almost touching her and he was, after all, a good trip.

The lady was nice, too. She lived in the small area of Belmont Drive where the ruling class lives. There was a stone fence around the property, and Shannon drove around it twice before discovering there really was an entrance. The gate was locked but a maid came running out to open it, and Shannon drove down the gently curved driveway amid the trees and flowers to the front door of the enormous house. The lady was on long distance telephone and would be out shortly, the maid informed her. She was really a snobby maid and treated Shannon with the disdain which is a taxi-driver's due. Shannon walked around the front yard which looked like a park, all landscaped and amazingly beautiful, and thought about the fact that there were no trees in the East End. She expected the lady to be as snobby as the maid, but the ruling class leaves that sort of thing to their servants and she was a very charming woman. She could be so charming only because the maid had been there first to make sure Shannon knew her place. It was a very convenient arrangement.

There are no trees in the East End. The Indian couple got in at the Columbia stand. The woman told Shannon they wanted a $5 ride but the man said, no, a $10 ride. They were both in their 60s. Shannon said she was off in half an hour and could only give them a $5 ride, unless they wanted another cab. The man gave her $10 and she gave him $5 in change.

Where do you want to go? Shannon asked.

Anywhere.

A tour, like?

Yeah.

Where have you been, so I won't take you to places you've already seen?

Port Alice, the woman said. We came down here and we haven't been anywhere but around here. The Balmoral Hotel.

Nowhere else?

I was in Stanley Park once, the man explained, it was when I got rolled. I woke up in Stanley Park and didn't know where I was. My head hurt.

Christ. How long have you been in Vancouver?

Three months. Now we're going home. There are no trees here, no grass, only drunks and pimps. You can't tell the seasons are changing except by whether or not drunks freeze on the streets.

Okay, Shannon said, Gastown first, since it's on our way.

They liked Gastown, giggling at the old buildings and leather shops and beaded belts. The business district of West Pender and Georgia didn't impress them, though Shannon explained this was where all the money was, and this was why all the Indians were poor, and why there were no trees on Columbia Street.

They did, however, ask her to drive closer to the Bayshore. The old man was not impressed, but the old woman said maybe the ass's yacht was there, giggling.

What?

The ass's. Jackie's husband.

Oh, him.

Then they drove to Stanley Park, halfway around it and over the Lion's Gate bridge, then back and around the other side of the park to Beach Avenue. Shannon was going to be late and it was getting to be more like a $10 ride after all, but they were happy in the park.

The leaves are all lush and green like this at home in the summer, the old woman said. I wasn't sure it was summer. There are no trees on Columbia Street. Here, the trees would turn all red and golden in the fall. We're going home.

Take a good look, the man said. English Bay. So you can say you've seen it.

I've seen it, the old woman said, and now we're going home.

Normally Shannon knew better than to argue with people from the Bayshore. The ones who stayed at the Georgia or the Hotel Vancouver were all right. They thought socialism was an interesting theory, but felt it hadn't too much to do with them. The people from the Bayshore were more class conscious, and they found socialism and women's liberation to be personally threatening.

While her fare was getting in the cab, Shannon was explaining to a woman how to get to the airport. He ordered Shannon to stop doing so immediately and take him to the airport, which she did, saying yes sir and touching her non-existent hat.

How do you like your job? he asked. Shannon smiled at him brightly, the way one is supposed to. Are you married? he asked then.

I don't answer that question and think my private life is my own business, Shannon replied.

This alerted him immediately. Oh, really? he said. And what do you think about the election?

NDP will win.

They won't win! If they do, they will drive industry from B.C.

Will they? Most B.C. industry is based on mining and logging. So if industry leaves, they will have to take the trees and mountains with them. As for the rest, sweatshops should be driven out of business.

He kept telling Shannon, all the way to the airport, that she didn't understand, and how did she think money was made. She said she knew, by exploiting people in developing countries. But he bled for poor old widows and demanded of Shannon how she would handle pension plans. He demanded to know what she would do for all the people she knew who were holding stocks. She said she didn't know any, about which he was incredulous. Everybody knew someone who held stocks, but Shannon cast about in her mind with great care and concluded that not one person of her acquaintance held stocks, and her passenger nearly choked with amazement. She thought, without feeling it was necessary to tell him, that he was partly right, and that Social Democrats who were seriously out to reform capitalism without changing the economics of it, could indeed cause a few problems.

The man recovered and continued his tirade. He said he was responsible for the lives of 1200 people and he paid them more than they were worth and some of them were useless, but he couldn't fire them. If he fired them or reduced their wages, they might talk to socialist cabbies and there would be no end of trouble. It had been a long time since anyone had taken her seriously enough to consider her dangerous, and for the sake of those 1200 people, Shannon made him carry his own bags and refused his tip with surly indifference.

It was a full moon, which is why the man had been inspired to talk, as normally those kind of people don't talk to cab-drivers.

When Shannon got back downtown, a man from the Clifton told Shannon he was almost 50 and his girlfriend was only 20. She preferred him to younger men because young men beat women up. Shannon asked him if women were being beat up more often in the last few years, but he didn't think so and thought that women were always beat up. He was a furniture mover and pretended he was only doing it for exercise because otherwise he couldn't stand the job. Shannon told him most workers had to fantasize something like that because most jobs were horrible, and she herself imagined she was a writer to make the days tolerable.

It was a full moon and all the crazies were out. A young man of about 25 told Shannon he had taken 16 Valiums. She didn't reply. What will happen to me? he asked.

You'll probably feel sleepy.

Will I die?

No.

How about 16 Valiums and six 292s?

You won't feel very good. Want to go to St. Paul's? I'm sure the Skillett doesn't want to look after no parasite.

Will I die?

No. Do you want to die?

I don't care. I only took them to see what it would feel like. You should experience everything. I've had all sorts of other highs, but never before have I taken 16 Valiums and six 292s. You should experience everything.

Even being dumb?

It's not dumb. Don't knock it if you haven't tried it.

Tell you what, I'll drive you to the middle of the bridge and you jump off and experience swimming after 16 Valiums and six 292s.

Do you think I'm crazy?

No, you're just stupid.

Conversation on the radio reached new levels of inanity that morning of the full moon.

There's a two car accident on the Granville Bridge. People lying all over the street.

Where?

Granville Bridge.

Granville Bridge?

Granville Bridge.

Which way?

Southbound.

I was over just a few minutes ago and there wasn't anyone.

Well, there's people lying on the road.

When did it happen?

Yesterday, you dummy.

I was just over a few minutes ago and there wasn't anyone lying on the street.

There's no people there now either, a third voice said. There's been an accident and there is two cars sitting sideways, but the only people here are walking around.

Well, there was people lying on the pavement a few minutes ago.

A fat and drunk man got out of a car at Broadway and Burrard and fell into Shannon's cab.

Never again, he said, holding his head.

That's what they all say. I've already heard that six times this morning.

I used to be an athlete. Gone to pot. Never again.

All athletes go to pot.

It was when I was in Korea.

What did you go there for?

To prove I was a man. Proved I was nothing. His head fell forward on his large chest.

September 1972

Shannon's owner had put a radio in the car since he drove it himself on weekends, so she could listen to the Canada-Soviet hockey games. Most passengers, however, objected, so she had to turn it down whenever there were people in the car. Those who were interested seemed quite pleased to see the NHL being cut down during the series.

One morning during the series, Eddie and Jim found her having breakfast at K-G's and sat down with her. Most drivers had decided she was a lesbian, so they didn't maul her any more and just treated her like another driver. It was a great relief, and now she could be friendly or contemptuous or whatever she felt with other drivers without fear. When anyone asked her, she denied being a lesbian but without conviction, because it was so much easier when they thought she was a lesbian. She thought that if there was one she wanted to sleep with, they could get to be friends first because he wouldn't know for a while that she was lusting after his body. There were none, however, that she could see herself as having any kind of lasting relationship with.

Eddie and Jim both said it was a great thing the Russians were winning because the strongest team should win. Shannon thought the fascist philosophy was a very comfortable one. You simply cheered for the winner, who proved by virtue of winning that he should have won. No analysis, no doubts, no troubling moral questions.

Having cleared that up, Eddie and Jim began talking about the election and said they would vote Social Credit because that seemed to them in the winning tradition. They also told Shannon they supported Nixon's policy.

Which policy? The one he says or the one he does?

Bombing the north, Eddie explained.

They oughta wipe them out. Jim added.

But they're losing, Shannon said. What about the troop with-drawals?

That's a lie, Jim said. The troops are only going to Thailand and Cambodia. Same difference as them being in Vietnam. In the meantime, they're wiping Laos off the map and destroying the north. Wiping them out.

They ought to invade the north, Eddie said.

But then China would get messed up in it, Jim protested.

Bomb them, too, Eddie said. What the hell. Who'd miss them? Would you miss 500 million chinks?

No, Jim replied, I wouldn't.

They can't invade the north, Shannon said, because their soldiers won't go. The soldiers know when they're beat, and everybody knows they're beat. I'd better leave here before my brain rots. I'd better quit driving cab, too, because it rots your brain.

All morning her passengers also spouted racism at her, and seemed surprised she objected. Hardly anyone else objected. Even hippies told her the same things. But then hippies had changed over the years. The most ragged and dirty ones would have a huge roll of bills in their jeans, which they had presum-ably made in the dope trade, or maybe they just dressed hippie some days and the rest of the time wore mod suits and wigs and were junior executives. One group told Shannon they owned several race horses.

You either got racism or plain inanity. The two drunks were going to Shaughnessy Hospital. The first one could walk pretty well, so he came out fast and then they waited for the second one. He finally made it, falling into the back of the cab, and Shannon drove off towards Shaughnessy.

I got lost, the drunker one said. So many hallways. Fucking halls. What do they need so many doors for?

There's a lot of halls, all right.

Fucking halls. Nother one every time. Dunno what they need so many halls for? Wado they need so many halls for? Never thought I'd find it. Fucking halls.

I thought you were coming right behind me.

Fucking halls. I was walking down halls. Fucking doors. Couldn't find it. Wado they need so many for? Nother hall, nother hall. All doors. Halls with doors. Doors with halls.

Look, Johnny, when we get there, you sit in the TV room and I'll go visit the old man.

Is he sick?

Yeah, if I don't see him this week, I won't see him, know what I mean?

He's gonna die.

That's why I want you to sit in the TV room. Half an hour. I'll come and get you.

What?

You sit there. I'll go visit the old man and you wait in the TB ward.

Sick, is he?

Yeah, so you wait and I'll go see him. Then I'll come and get you.

See that church?

That one?

The church.

Which church?

That one.

That one?

That church.

That's a synagogue.

Yeah. That one.

That's not a church, that's a synagogue.

That church. My wife.

Was your wife Jewish?

Dead. Married and buried.

In that church?

Dear heart, she's been dead such a long time. Married and buried. Dear heart. Dead, dead, dead. Dear heart. Christ, what an asshole she was. Dead, dead, dead.

Yeah, Johnny, that's why I want you to sit in the TB ward. I'll go see the old man and you sit there and wait. Half an hour, no more.

Dead, dead, dead.

September 2, 1972

The first two people were hookers who had never heard of the election, which more or less put it in its proper perspective.

The third person was a man from the Yale, muttering of blood and machine guns and East Germany. He didn't have the money to pay the fare. In the middle of all that, he told Shannon women were the weaker sex.

You creep, she said. Sitting there crying because you might be hurt. Having to beg because you drank up all your money. Oh yeah, you're strong all right. Snivelling and begging and unable to walk. He started to cry and Shannon never did know what to do when men cried.

The next passenger was a woman who was pleased the NDP had won because then Gaglardi had lost and all Italians were crooks. Shannon wondered whether the NDP supporters were, on the average, more degenerate than their opposition. There didn't seem to be much of a contest. At least the woman paid the fare.

After that, Shannon got some businessmen in the distillery business going to the Terminal Club. They said there were some at the Terminal Club who were pleased about the NDP victory because of the patronage practiced by Bennett and his government. They expected the NDP to be the same, only honester.

A man from the British Properties going to the airport was much more pessimistic about it. He expected there would be many changes and none of them good. He was a mining developer and the NDP had always been vehemently opposed to mining in parks.

Parks are more important than mines, Shannon told him. Where would you take your kids if there were no parks? I know, you don't need to take your kids anywhere because your own house has a yard as big as a park, but not everyone can afford a private park.

The man told Shannon it was attitudes like hers that retarded progress, and she asked him Steinbeck's question, which is how come progress looks so much like destruction?

The little old lady didn't know anything about the election. She was 75 years old and was going to visit her sister in Surrey. The sister lived next door to some people who didn't like children.

How could anyone not like children?

They always were funny.

Do you like children?

Oh yes, in spite of how my husband was. I was only 17 when I was married, and way back then nobody told you anything. Kids know more now at six than I did when I was 17. My husband was very bad-tempered. We lived on a farm first, in Saskatchewan that was, and I was alone most of the time, and I even used to look forward to him coming home at first, but then I'd get nervous thinking what have I done wrong now.

I didn't know anything so I had the first baby right away. She was a nice baby and when I got pregnant again right away, I was pleased, thinking the next one might be a boy and then I'd have one of each. It wasn't so lonely, and she was such a nice baby. But my husband went to the drugstore and came back with some brown pills he said I had to take. He used to throw me across the room whenever I didn't do what he said, and you know how it was then, and I was very young and I did whatever he said. I took several of the pills while he was watching, but they only made me sick. In those days, with stoves and heaters, it was much easier to get rid of stuff than it is now, and oh my, it did come in handy sometimes. I don't know what people do now. So I threw the pills, box and all, into the stove while he was out, and he kept asking me and I told him I had taken them all but that the pills didn't work for everyone, that part of it was true anyhow, they didn't work for everyone. I've never met anyone they did work for, but then you didn't talk about it in those days, you know how it was. That baby was a girl, too, and she was ever such a nice baby.

My boy was born in the hospital. My, that was easy. With all the other babies I had such a hard time, but that one was in hospital. That was when I was living with my mother in Regina, when my boy was born. My husband was away for a year. My husband's brother worked for a telephone company and my husband took a night school course. He wasn't stupid, my husband wasn't, but oh my, he was bad-tempered. His brother told him where to apply for a job, and he got a job in Alberta. It was supposed to be for only a few months, so it wasn't worth the whole family going out there. So he moved me and my children to my mother's in Regina and went himself and then the job was changed to six months, then a few more months. He didn't come home for a whole year.

That was the only happy year of my married life.

November 1972

What's the baby going to be when she grows up?

She'll be a person, Evelyn said.

How will she express her personhood?

She'll go to university, Bradley said, and be somebody. I'll have to go to work for a couple of years to send her, but what the hell. Hey, Punkin, do you want to be somebody?

No, the baby replied. I want to be a mother.

A mother!!!??? Oh Lord, Bradley moaned, betrayed by my own offspring. Shafted by the fruit of my loins. Child, did I not sing to you? Revolutionary songs. Women's Liberation songs.

Maybe I'll be a tiger then.

You can't be a tiger, you have to be a person.

I can do whatever I want, the baby said, dancing in the middle of the kitchen.

Okay, be a tiger, I don't care. I'll even come to visit you in your cage. Be a mother then, but don't ask me to babysit my grandchildren. What the hell, do ask me. Being a mother is better than working for the CPR. And certainly better than working for Office Overload. I'll be a grandmother. Be whatever you want. Just don't drive cab, like this jerk. Why don't you get a decent job, Shannon?

There are no decent jobs. How about saying "information" 30 times a minute or whatever their quota is? How about filing for 45 years? Maybe there will be a revolution in her lifetime and she will be able to do meaningful work.

Garbage, Bradley said. No work is meaningful.

Come on. Being a mother would be tremendous work in another society. You're thinking of jobs. You hate all your jobs, but at home you fix cars and fix the plumbing and you don't hate that, because it's proper work, not some stupid job where you never see the results of your work. I'd be a mother, you know, in another society. Where it was an honourable occupation and paid for a comfortable life for me and the children. Where the children had something other than wars and violence and racism and pollution to grow up to. Well, you know all that, you've described to me often enough the frantic methods of birth control you use so there won't be any more kids.

What about Evelyn? Bradley demanded. Evelyn only does anything when she's forced to and she can't do any of it right. She either burns everything or it's raw. She's always late for work. If she wasn't forced to do anything, she'd just sit with her mouth open.

I would not, Evelyn said, don't be so stupid.

Okay then, what would you do? Huh? What would you do?

I don't know.

See? Bradley said to Shannon with great satisfaction.

Don't pick on Evelyn, she said. There was a time when Evelyn was self-motivated. She got married too young. Girls aren't allowed to develop fast and we were going at our own slow speed and then you came along and seduced her or however it all happened. Before that, we were going to be really great and do all sorts of things. What were we going to be, Evelyn?

I don't remember.

Well, it doesn't matter. I assure you, Bradley, she was going to be something. Pour her more vodka, the poor thing. Whatever that something was, it didn't include incompetent housewifery, broken alarm clocks, sickly babies, or drunken husbands. I was going to be rich and famous. But, see, we are ruled by our lives, we don't control what happens to us.

How would you change all that if there was a revolution?

I wouldn't change anything. You don't have dictators like in Russia and call that revolution. I only get some say in what happens to cab-drivers, that's what workers' control means. So we get lunch breaks and go to the toilet like everybody else. Workers now get paid according to the amount of capital investment the boss made. If the machines are expensive, the workers get paid a lot so they won't be surly and either deliberately or by negligence break machines. But in the cab business, the price of the car is the least of the owners' expenses so they don't care if they have a bunch of surly, half-mad operators.

And everybody will work, but only a few days a week. No more slag heaps of old people, no more refrigerators for young people. This will increase the work force and nobody will have to work very much. I'll work 16 hours a week like everybody else and get paid $500 a month. Once a week there will be a meeting of all the cab-drivers who want to come and decide policy. Just like the directors' meetings, only we will all be directors. Just as we'll all be owners. At these meetings we will make new rules and change old ones, reprimand or praise each other as necessary, hire new people and all that. And we'll even pass resolutions on rapid transit and pollution and be terribly socially conscious and decide the banks can't buy the Caribbean and that sort of thing, because we'll have time to read and discuss and decide. We'll have really long meetings, and have factional disputes, and be very passionate about it all because it's more fun that way, and we won't always be tired.

We won't open people's doors for them. Even little old ladies who don't know how to open doors because nobody has ever allowed them to, will now be initiated into the mysteries of car-door-opening. We don't provide a service now, for fuck sake, we just pander to people's neuroses. It doesn't matter now if you never get people where they're going, as long as you carry their luggage and smile. Well, it won't be like that. It's an honourable job, cab-driving is, if you drive people from one place to another and don't pander to their neuroses. In fact, there won't be any personal servants at all. No waitresses, no secretaries. Just cooks and typists and like that. And everybody will carry their own luggage.

It sounds like a song, Bradley said. Everybody will carry their own luggage. And when you die you'll go to that great big highway in the sky where there's a flag on every corner and the traffic lights are always green.

Traffic lights always green, the baby sang, dancing in the middle of the kitchen.

It was an ordinary Saturday afternoon on a cold and clear fall day. It would snow later in the week, but now the sun was still shining and the wind had blown away the muck, so the city sparkled like a jewel beneath cold blue skies. I know that's an overused metaphor, but the city *did*. Like a diamond. It *did*. Or more like a bunch of diamonds. Sapphires, rubies, opals. That's what's wrong with the metaphor. The city sparkles like jewels.

An American couple with a child asked Shannon to take them on a tour of the city. It was a perfect morning for a tour. The man was an executive from Los Angeles, but they were nice people, so Shannon took them first to her favourite place in all of Vancouver, which was Little Mountain. She liked to show visitors the city, and she liked showing nice people Little Mountain.

The people gasped in appreciation as they stood above the garden looking out over the city and the bay. Shannon pointed out the river and Stanley Park and UBC and downtown. There was no one else at the park because it was cold, so they were the only people in the world and all four were gripped with exhilaration at the sight of so much beauty spread beneath them.

Since they were now all friends, the man wanted to know more about Canada, as this was their first visit to Canada.

I read your paper last night, he said, and there was a lot of stuff about foreign domination of the economy I couldn't understand. Why don't you people just throw the British out like we did?

The British? Shannon stared at him in amazement. There was a longish silence while both the man and woman looked uncomfortable, then Shannon said: The British Empire died some time ago.

Oh, the man said unhappily, it's American domination. Well, why don't you do something about that?

You know why. You said you were an executive for an oil company so you must know something. Vietnam objected to foreign domination and now their people are maimed and their land burned. The Dominican Republic objected and the Marines marched in. See, there's the border behind us. You've got the largest and most technological destructive force in the world, and your army would come marching across there, and your planes would destroy this city in minutes.

The man and the woman were nice people and they stared out at the city in shocked silence.

We're not like that, really, the man said at last.

Tell that to the Vietnamese.

What's going to happen?

I don't know. I think you're beat in Vietnam and I think the monstrous machine will slowly grind to a halt, only you've got a berserk ruling class and there's going to be yet a lot more destruction. But it will die, eventually. Here, I don't know what we'll do. Mostly we'll just wait, I guess. I don't know what else there is to do. I don't know how long it will take. You don't fight the ruling class at a time when it's certain they will win. I don't know. I think the taxi-drivers should get organized and demand to be treated as people with dignity. The women's movement here is more like a working-class movement, though the media is making what may be a successful attempt to destroy it by making out it's only so women can get to be executives. If that's all it is, or if women are convinced and brainwashed into thinking that's all it is, then a few women will be promoted into the middle class and that will leave the rest of us poorly paid and unorganized as before. And there's all this stuff about independent unions. If people are brainwashed into thinking it's only about being Canadian, then that will fail too. I don't know. Whatever happens, I think it will happen in Quebec first, but then they can't do it all by themselves either. I think taxi-drivers should get organized. I don't know what will happen in the end. There is no end.

The little boy had discovered the garden and was shouting for them to come and see, and the woman had gone to try and understand the sculpture. The man leaned against the rail looking out over the city and the mountains, purple and cold against the cold blue sky.

We're not like that really, he said again.

Don't be so innocent, Shannon said gently. An executive in the bloodiest empire in the history of the world has no right to be innocent. I drive a cab down there, so I have no illusions. I used to be a nice person. You can be nice still because you don't have to do your own dirty work, because the soldiers conscripted out of the ghettoes kill for you. Here, they hide in their Shaughnessy mansions and it's cops who kill Indians, and drunken degenerates who rape women for them. And your doped up kids cut a swath of destruction across the world on behalf of your oil company.

It is, of course, a waste of time to persuade the ruling class they are wrong, so maybe Shannon didn't say all that to the guy. He was only a young man and not very important anyway. Or maybe she did say it, but not like that. In any case, then she took the man over to show him the Henry Moore sculpture, and at the end of the tour he gave her a $5 tip, which he probably wouldn't have done if she had talked like that.

In the afternoon, Shannon got tangled up in the traffic around Woodward's for almost an hour while trying to extricate a drunk from the Palace Bar. She gave up and didn't even tell the despatcher she had a no-load because then he'd have given her another trip in the zone and it would take another half hour to get to it and then it might be another drunk who would decide he would stay for another beer after all, or a jerk going to Eaton's. Mad about the cab service. The cab service in the area around Woodward's, at UBC, and anywhere downtown during the rush hour and at night when the pubs closed, had been very poor if not non-existent for about a year already. Neither the cab owners nor City Hall knew what to do about it. Shannon knew, but nobody asked her.

She drove uptown and was eventually despatched to the Grosvenor. There they told her that the bellhop had gone up to get the luggage and she should wait in the car. She would have liked to wait in the warm lobby, but then people would have stared at her. She sat in the car for about ten minutes, thinking about how she hadn't made any money at all in the last hour and a half, till the luggage finally came downstairs.

The man was going to the Plaza 500 for $1.35. Shannon saw him give the bellhop $1, which was bad. The big tippers demanded service. She got out and put his bags in the trunk and closed his door, like a good servant. At the Plaza 500, she mucked about opening the trunk so she wouldn't have to open his door for him, but he just sat there, a big and healthy male, so she finally opened the door for him. She took his bags from the trunk and set them on the sidewalk, but he was already walking into the hotel. She picked up the bags, like a good servant, and followed him inside. Meekly. And smiled when he tipped her 65 cents. Pedestals and fragility have always been the privilege of middle and upper-middle-class women.

Then she got some hippies who couldn't all get together, so it was about ten minutes before they were all in the car, and in the meantime, traffic was backing up on 12th and everybody was blowing their horns.

The hippies were going to Georgia and Granville. The light at Georgia was red so she told them they could get out there, but it took so long to collect the money for the fare that the light changed and the traffic moved forward. Shannon told them to wait, though they called her names, but the light turned red again before she had time to get through it. When they were getting out, the driver behind her leaned on his horn.

There was a truck turning right onto Granville off Georgia around a construction fence; he got hooked against the fence and couldn't move, blocking all the southbound traffic and one lane of the northbound traffic. When the light turned green, Shannon let the first car in the blocked lane go ahead of her, which caused the driver behind her to lean on his horn and scream in a paroxysm of indignation. Shannon had got to the middle of the intersection, but he was still blowing his horn, so she stopped and watched the man's hysterical execution of his masculine role.

At the Hudson's Bay, there were a whole bunch of flags. A young man and woman were the most agile, so they got to the cab first and the other people waved their fists and yelled obscenities. The young man exclaimed that it was the second time that day he had seen a woman driver and wasn't it amazing. He said that about 20 times, so finally Shannon asked him if he'd never seen a woman before. He said that wasn't what he meant. She asked him to please not act as if he was at the zoo, and he said, but wasn't it *amazing* to see *two* women drivers in one day. Shannon didn't answer, so he asked her if she made much money. Shannon said not nearly enough for the shit she had to take, and then the young man thought he was being insulted and called her a bitch, though the woman with him tried to calm him down.

Shannon didn't take any more trips that day, feeling it was too dangerous. She went home and got awful drunk and talked to Bradley about it all, but the next morning she couldn't remember what she had said, except that she remembered saying she was proud of being a taxi-driver, and it was a good and honourable job, and why didn't people know more swear words so she wouldn't hear the same ones all the time.

But every morning is a new day, and the next morning Shannon was driving down Granville singing, and the city was sparkling like jewels beneath a cold blue sky. The mountain tops were covered with snow.

She took a lawyer type to the airport. He said he was going to Mexico. At the airport, she got his bags out of the trunk. There was a large bag and a camera case, which she slung over her shoulder. The lawyer type was standing on the sidewalk, waiting for his baggage, but Shannon walked right past him towards the entry door. Then she turned around, handed him the car keys, told him not to forget to check the oil, and continued into the airport. He ran after her and said, wait a minute, wait a minute, those are my bags.

They are? Shannon asked in mock surprise.

You're the cab-driver, he said, handing back her keys.

Well, isn't that amazing! she said, staring at the keys with suspicion while handing him his baggage. Tell me, how did a nice girl like me end up this way?

He rushed away, clutching his bag and camera. No sense of humour, those lawyer types.

Cab-driving is more honourable than lawyering, she yelled after him. Then she muttered to herself about lawyers and how, after the revolution, some jobs would be done away with, but cab-drivers are necessary in all societies.

Other current New Star titles

SMALL RAIN *by John Harris.* A college instructor leaves his wife and enters the world of emotional insecurity, financial worry, and self-doubt. A familiar story, but Harris's cool, clear-eyed view of how the world turns imbues his tales of academic, political, and sexual life in a northern boom-and-bust town with satiric humour and unusual twists. 140 pages. **$12.95 Cdn. / $9.95 U.S.**

NO WAY TO LIVE Poor Women Speak Out *by Sheila Baxter.* Fifty women talk about their poverty. Includes statistical information on poverty and women, as well as a directory of anti-poverty and women's groups in Canada. 231 pages. **$9.95**

HASTINGS AND MAIN Stories from an Inner City Neighbourhood *Interviews by Laurel Kimbley; Edited by Jo-Ann Canning-Dew.* Reminiscences of twenty long-time residents of Vancouver's Downtown Eastside upset many of the stereotypes about "skid road". 158 pages. **$9.95**

JAPAN The Blighted Blossom *by Roy Thomas.* A popular portrait of contemporary Japan. Stripping away the façade of prosperous success the Japanese have erected between themselves and the West, Thomas scrutinizes the high price this "rich nation of poor people" has paid for success in its work life, family life, corruption-riddled democratic institutions, and educational system.
300 pages. **$25.95 Cdn. / $20.95 U.S.**

SHRINK RESISTANT The Struggle Against Psychiatry in Canada *Edited by Bonnie Burstow and Don Weitz.* Through interviews, journal entries, poetry, graphics, and personal narratives, 40 current and former psychiatric inmates relate their experiences inside the walls of mental hospitals and at the hands of psychiatrists. 360 pages. **$11.95**

A PEOPLE IN ARMS *by Marie Jakober.* A dramatic novel of love and revolution, set in Nicaragua. Continues the story begun in her 1985 novel, *Sandinista.*
303 pages. **$9.95**

THE SUPREME COURT OF CANADA DECISION ON ABORTION *Edited by Shelagh Day and Stan Persky.* The complete text of the Supreme Court's historic decision in the Morgentaler case striking down Section 251 of the Criminal Code — Canada's abortion law. Includes a Commentary by Shelagh Day and an Introduction by Stan Persky. 225 pages. **$5.95**

To order, send cheque or money order to New Star Books Ltd. Price shown includes shipping & handling.

For a free catalogue containing a complete list of New Star titles, write to the address below:

New Star Books Ltd.
2504 York Avenue
Vancouver, B.C.
CANADA V6K 1E3